WITH MALICE

(A Maeve Sharp Mystery—Book 1)

Rylie Dark

Rylie Dark

Bestselling author Rylie Dark is author of the SADIE PRICE FBI SUSPENSE THRILLER series, comprising six books; of the CARLY SEE FBI SUSPENSE THRILLER series, comprising six books; of the MIA NORTH FBI SUSPENSE THRILLER series, comprising six books (and counting); of the MORGAN STARK FBI SUSPENSE THRILLER series, comprising five books; of the HAILEY ROCK FBI SUSPENSE THRILLER series, comprising five books (and counting); of the TARA STRONG MYSTERY series, comprising five books (and counting); of the ALEX QUINN FBI SUSPENSE THRILLER series, comprising five books (and counting); and of the MAEVE SHARP FBI SUSPENSE THRILLER, comprising five books (and counting).

An avid reader and lifelong fan of the mystery and thriller genres, Rylie loves to hear from you, so please feel free to visit www.ryliedark.com to learn more and stay in touch.

ISBN: 978-1-0943-7922-7

BOOKS BY RYLIE DARK

MAEVE SHARP FBI SUSPENSE THRILLER
WITH MALICE (Book #1)
WITH ENVY (Book #2)
WITH VENGEANCE (Book #3)
WITH RAGE (Book #4)
WITH YOU (Book #5)

ALEX QUINN SUSPENSE THRILLER
FIRST, MURDER (Book #1)
SECOND, DEATH (Book #2)
THIRD, ENVY (Book #3)
FOURTH, LUST (Book #4)
FIFTH, WRATH (Book #5)

TARA STRONG MYSTERY
GIRL WITHOUT A CHANCE (Book #1)
GIRL WITHOUT A HOME (Book #2)
GIRL WITHOUT A TRACE (Book #3)
GIRL WITHOUT A NAME (Book #4)
GIRL WITHOUT A PRAYER (Book #5)

HAILEY ROCK FBI SUSPENSE THRILLER
BEHIND YOU (Book #1)
BESIDE YOU (Book #2)
AFTER YOU (Book #3)
WATCHING YOU (Book #4)
JUDGING YOU (Book #5)

SADIE PRICE FBI SUSPENSE THRILLER
ONLY MURDER (Book #1)
ONLY RAGE (Book #2)
ONLY HIS (Book #3)
ONLY ONCE (Book #4)
ONLY SPITE (Book #5)
ONLY MADNESS (Book #6)

MIA NORTH FBI SUSPENSE THRILLER
SEE HER RUN (Book #1)
SEE HER HIDE (Book #2)
SEE HER SCREAM (Book #3)
SEE HER VANISH (Book #4)
SEE HER GONE (Book #5)
SEE HER DEAD (Book #6)

CARLY SEE FBI SUSPENSE THRILLER
NO WAY OUT (Book #1)
NO WAY BACK (Book #2)
NO WAY HOME (Book #3)
NO WAY LEFT (Book #4)
NO WAY UP (Book #5)
NO WAY TO DIE (Book #6)

MORGAN STARK FBI SUSPENSE THRILLER
TOO LATE (Book #1)
TOO CLOSE (Book #2)
TOO FAR GONE (Book #3)
TOO LOST (Book #4)
TOO BROKEN (Book #5)

PROLOGUE

Richard stormed down the massive top floor hallway of the luxury hotel, determined to put an end to this. The owner's daughter had been making his life hell, holed up in the penthouse suite for a month, partying all night, forcing guests to flee, and making his staff miserable. As manager, the guest complaints all fell on him.

Not anymore. Finally, the owner had given him the OK to ask his daughter to vacate. The little brat wouldn't answer the room phone, of course. Or her cell phone. Or his texts.

Now this was the only way.

He approached the door, his card key out, ready to use it if he had to.

He knocked sharply, three times.

He looked out the window while he waited for an answer, the Las Vegas skyline sparkling in the distance. *The Azure Heights Grand Resort* was the crown jewel of the Vegas strip, and he wouldn't have the hotel's reputation ruined by one spoiled little girl.

Still, no answer.

"Juliette!" he yelled. "This is Richard Simon. The hotel manager. I need you to open this door *now.*" Richard was past patient, after fielding months' worth of complaints about noise, partying, trash, and destroyed hotel property.

The silence on the other side of the door was deafening. Richard felt the beginning of a headache at the base of his neck. He knew the owner's daughter was in there, but why wouldn't she answer the door? He knocked again, this time louder than before.

Silence greeted Richard's words, just as he expected. He took a deep breath and tried to calm his nerves. Dealing with Juliette was never easy, but he had to do it.

"Juliette, I'm not going to ask you again. Open this door right now!" He continued to knock, but still no answer. He could feel his temper rising with each passing second. His heart began to race, and he could feel his face turning red.

Richard waited a few moments before knocking again, but still, there was no answer. He gritted his teeth in frustration, knowing he couldn't let this slide anymore.

Finally, he decided to use his card key.

He swiped the card through the lock, but it didn't work. She must have changed the locks.

Richard felt his face go hot with anger. How did she even get permission to do that? He reached into his pocket for the master key card that worked on all the doors in the hotel. It was for emergencies only, but he figured that this warranted its use.

He swiped it again, and with a beep, the lock clicked open. Richard pushed the door open slowly, peering inside. The room was dimly lit, the curtains drawn. He could hear music blaring from somewhere inside.

"Juliette?" he called out, stepping into the room. As his eyes adjusted to the darkness, he saw her lying on the king-sized bed, sound asleep. Richard never understood how people could sleep so late into the day, or through such loud music. She was dressed in a silk robe that barely covered her, and her blonde hair spread around her in a halo.

He shook his head, trying to clear his thoughts. He was here to do a job. He couldn't let her terrorize the other guests any longer.

But as he looked closer, he froze.

There was something strange about her body. It seemed too....stiff. Her skin color, it seemed too...pale.

Almost blue.

Richard's heart raced as he moved closer to the bed, his eyes fixed on the still form lying there. He knew what he had to do, but he couldn't bring himself to do it. He reached out a trembling hand and placed it on Juliette's shoulder, giving it a gentle shake.

"Juliette?" he whispered, all the anger drained as he wondered what Mr. Cavendish would say if something happened to his beautiful, beloved daughter. But there was no response. He tried again, but still, there was nothing. Panic set in as he leaned in closer, searching for any signs of life.

But there was nothing.

Richard dropped his key card and stumbled away from the figure lying before him.

Juliette Cavendish was dead.

CHAPTER ONE

Special Agent Maeve Sharp drove up the dusty drive to the trailer park where her father had spent the past eight years. She looked out over the barren Nevada landscape. The Las Vegas suburbs had disappeared miles back, and now there was nothing but sandy earth and the beating sun. Even though she had not been back to her home state in years, the dusty smell and hazy sky were familiar to Maeve.

She had spent the last five years in Quantico, Virginia, working at the FBI headquarters as a detective before her mother's failing health and brother's legal problems finally forced her to return. After long years of being away, pretending she didn't have a family at all, the place felt different.

But she had come here for the reunion she had been dreading the most.

She passed the other mobile homes, baked by the Nevada sun, with rusting walls in front of small lawns of rocks, sand, and cacti.

Her father's trailer was pushed back from the main road, and she had to pull her old Camry onto the dirt road to get there. She parked next to his old pickup, and tried to look in the window, which had been blocked by curtains. On the front door, there was a sign that read, "come back with a warrant."

Maeve got out of the car and slid her sunglasses to the top of her head. *Never thought I'd come back here,* she thought, with a grimace on her lips. She remembered the day her father moved in, in spite of her urging him not to. He threw out half his belongings, and only kept a few old clothes and casefiles from his days as a cop.

She knew that the isolation wouldn't be good for him, that it wouldn't help him solve his problems, but he insisted it was for "financial purposes."

That was, of course, a lie. This dusty trailer was his way of hiding from the world.

At the very least, he would be happy to see her… wouldn't he? He'd hug her like he used to when he got home from work and found her playing in her room. She stood for a long moment, next to his rusted pickup truck, wondering if she should go in.

What did the two of them have to say to each other?

The door opened before she could knock, and there he stood, a scowl on his face. He was tall, with a large stomach and a long, graying ponytail. His long beard was flecked with white and brown, and his dark eyes were set deep in his weathered face. He was wearing a dirty white t-shirt, and a pair of torn, dirty jeans.

He was unrecognizable from the man she had grown up with. He had never been cuddly or warm, but still he had never been like *this*, with so little care for his own health or hygiene. For most of her childhood, he had been a clean-cut cop who never bent the rules, who spent his career trying to clean up Vegas. But that was before life collapsed around him— around all of them— and he retreated here.

At first he said nothing, just looked her up and down with a frown on his face. And then, in a low, grumble, "It must be important if you had to come all the way from Quantico." Was that a hint of irritation in his voice that Maeve detected?

Maeve stepped back and put her hands on her hips. She forced herself to remain calm, upbeat almost. She knew that this visit would be hard. A lot had changed in the five years since she had last returned home. She had not expected some sort of tearful reunion, but she had hoped for something. A hug, even a simple 'hello.' Something to indicate that he cared about his daughter, but now she wasn't so sure that he did.

"Dad," she began, but he cut her off.

"What do you want?"

"For a start, you could invite me inside." She quickly realized that this visit would not be what she hoped for.

He turned back to the dark interior of the trailer and nodded for her to follow him.

Inside, the smell of stale beer and cigarettes hit Maeve's nose. The trailer was dark and cramped, with a small kitchen and a tiny living room, with a faded green couch, a coffee table, and a small TV. The sink was piled with dirty dishes and old whiskey bottles. A black curtain had been pulled across the only window.

Maeve looked around and took a sharp breath. She turned away so that he wouldn't see the frown forming on her face.

Maeve had hoped to find him in better shape than this. It broke her heart to see how far he had fallen, but what hurt more was knowing that she couldn't help him. There were bigger issues in their broken family. In his years of living off the grid like a ghost, his living situation had only deteriorated, while Maeve's visits became less and less frequent.

The walls were covered pictures from old case files, the ones that he had never managed to solve. Victim's pale faces were plastered on the walls. He caught Maeve looking at them and scowled.

Maeve's gaze landed on the familiar pictures of Veronica— her younger sister.

It shocked her to see her sister's face smiling back from the images attached to police reports and newspaper clippings.

She had disappeared from the Vegas strip at age 18 without a trace.

Of all the cases he never solved, it was the disappearance of his own daughter that haunted him.

Maeve looked at her sister's dark hair and light eyes smiling back at her.

"That's private," he said, stepping in between her and the wall of cases. "Didn't come all this way just to see me, did you SA Sharp?" He said in a mocking tone, taking a cigarette from his pocket and lighting it.

Maeve forced herself not to cough in the billowing cloud of smoke. It hurt to hear him say that. She thought, in a way, that she had been following in his footsteps, that maybe he could be proud of her.

She pursed her lips, knowing he wouldn't take well what she had to say next.

"I moved back. Three weeks ago." She had to work hard to keep her voice even, informative, telling him that the decision had already been made.

He rolled his eyes. "Never thought you'd come back here of all places. You had a hell of a career ahead of you."

Maeve's heart sank. Of all the members of her family, she and her father had been the closest. They were both natural rule followers, hard workers, and hungry to make sure that those who hurt other people faced justice. She had always looked up to him, even though he was never around. He was the reason that she chose to become a detective. And now he didn't even want her around.

"Trust me, I didn't want to," she answered, her voice getting cold.

"Why the hell did you come back, then?" There was a sharpness in his voice that made Maeve uneasy, like he was trying to get her to leave.

Maeve leaned on the table, not wanting to say what she was about to say, so she just spit it out.

"I didn't come back for *you*. What would be the point of that? You don't even want to see me."

He gave another low growl.

“I came back for Mom.” Maeve’s tone turned hard, angry, even though she didn’t want to give him the satisfaction of knowing he upset her. “I want you to come and visit her.”

He gave a rueful chuckle, laughing at the ridiculousness of the idea. “No,” he said. “I can’t see her again.”

"I want you to do this for me, Dad. Before it's too late."

"Too late? She's already dead, sis. Been dead to me for years," he said, chuckling again. He took another long drag of his cigarette.

Maeve took a deep breath and looked down at her hands. She didn’t want to be the one to break the news.

"She's gotten much worse, Dad. And I don't think she has much time left."

No matter how bitter he was, that news seemed to strike a chord. He looked down at the table, and then up at his daughter.

"How long?"

Maeve shrugged. "Hard to say," she answered. "I asked the doctors, and they said maybe she has a few months. A year, tops."

Four lines appeared on her father's forehead. The divorce was a messy one. Maeve didn't think that her parents had spoken since the day they signed the papers, but to Maeve that didn't mean that he shouldn’t be there for her now. After all that their family had gone through, he owed this last thing to her mother.

She set her jaw, and braced herself for the words she knew she had to say.

"I don't mean to tell you how to live your life. But I think it's time for you to make peace with her." Even as she spoke, she felt the weight of all that had happened in their family, and the guilt she carried for hiding from it for so long. Her voice began to crack, but she forced the feeling down.

He looked up at her, his eyes bloodshot. He looked like he hadn't slept in days.

"I can't do that," he shook his head. Could his tone be remorseful? No, Maeve decided. He wasn’t capable of that. "I can't."

Maeve sighed, giving up for the present moment. She wanted to throw one of his old beer bottles at him.

Of course he responded this way. Why did she let herself think that he could put the past behind him? That he could be there for her mother now that she needed him? Even when they had needed him as kids, he was never there. He was always off solving a case that was more important than their family.

She wondered if she would end up this way too. If years of seeing the worst in people would leave her this bitter, cold, with nowhere else to go but a dusty trailer park.

"You been to see that deadbeat brother of yours yet?" he murmured, as Maeve turned away.

"Not yet," she admitted, noting the intentional change of subject. She had been dreading this part of the visit to her father most, so she chose to get it out of the way.

"Maybe you could start there, help the kid stay out of the can."

"Your living arrangements aren't much better," Maeve said under her breath. "Besides, we both know that you're the only one who can do something for him. You're the one who is old pals with the DA."

"Don't even..."

"Maybe you could try. I bet if you asked, he would get a reduced sentence."

He shook his head again. "Let the kid learn. I get him out now, then he'll just land back in jail in a few months. That brother of yours, he's always making trouble."

Maeve's hands tightened into fists, so tight that her fingernails bit into her palms. Not wanting to bring up old wounds with his ex-wife was one thing, but abandoning his own son?

"You get a job with L.V.P.D.?" he asked. "I guess you finally wanted to follow in your old man's footsteps, huh?" he gave another half-hearted chuckle.

"I took a job at the Las Vegas field office." She replied, trying not to show him how hurt she was. "I'm still FBI."

"Field office, huh? I thought you were going to be a profiler."

"I still am," she replied firmly.

"But you decided to get back to your roots? Go back to working with the rookies?"

She shrugged. Of course, this had been her fear too, that the move would stunt her career and cost her the promotion to profiler that she had been gunning for since her first day at the academy.

"It's temporary," she said, as much to herself as to him. "I'm here to take care of Mom. If her doctors are right, then I'll be back at Quantico soon enough." As much as Maeve hated the thought of losing her mom, she knew that as soon as she was gone, she would move back east, where her career was waiting for her. This was just a brief interlude.

"Good," he snapped, and she could hear the venom in his voice. "Don't need you here anyway."

Maeve turned away so he wouldn't see her roll her eyes.

"I'm not going to see your mother. If you want to dredge up the past, be my guest. But I'm not going to do it with you."

Unable to deal with his attitude, Maeve stood up to go.

She waited for a reaction. A plea for her not to go, an apology, even a half-baked one, but no response came. Maeve felt stupid for coming here, for hoping that her father could change, even just a small amount, now that her family needed to come together.

"I should go," she said, moving to the door.

"Fine. Who needs you?" he muttered.

"Fine!" Maeve snapped, digging her car keys out of her pocket. "Stay here and rot for all I care."

She stormed out the door, and it snapped closed behind her before he could follow her out. She yanked her car door open and then sped away down the road, leaving a trail of dust kicked up behind her. As she looked at the trailer in the rear-view mirror, she saw her father wandering after her.

Tears threatened to run down her face. She felt a lump forming in her throat.

But she couldn't let herself cry.

I don't need him, she thought, her knuckles turning white as she gripped the steering wheel and sped down the highway, towards Nevada State Penitentiary.

It was time to see her brother. She could only hope that this reunion would be better than the last one, but with her brother's constant struggling, she wasn't so sure.

CHAPTER TWO

When Maeve pulled through the security gate into the parking lot of the prison, her father's words still rang in her ears. This place was almost as familiar to her as the trailer park, as it had been her brother's part-time home for the better part of a decade. Her twin was always getting himself into trouble, accidentally or otherwise.

He was currently in the middle of a three-year stint for possession of meth. Before that, it had been breaking and entering… the list went on.

Maeve followed procedure, and did exactly what the prison guards told her, as she unloaded her pockets onto an x-ray conveyor belt and walked through a metal detector. The guards nodded at her, and she was allowed to pass.

The sound of the security buzzer rang in her ears when she was finally allowed into the visitation room. The room was long and narrow, cut in half by a plexiglass window, lined with booths for talking to the prisoners on the other side.

He was already waiting for her at one of the booths.

She felt uneasy as she crossed the room. She clenched her jaw and pushed the fear away. She hated seeing him like this. To her, he was still the kid she grew up with—maybe a little stupid at times but not a hardened criminal. She had to be strong for him and not look as worried as she felt.

She had to be there for him now, since their mother couldn't and their father refused. She was all he had left.

And in a way, he was the same for her.

David looked so different in prison-orange, with sunken cheeks and mangy hair. Maeve hadn't seen him since her most recent visit five years ago, right before he got kicked out of a half-way house. She had been in the middle of a double homicide during the trial, and couldn't manage to find the time off to come visit him.

Of course, she called him every now and again.

Still, it was different to see him in person.

She mustered an encouraging smile from somewhere deep down, and sank into the chair opposite him. She picked up the phone, which felt grimy in her hand.

"Hey, sis," he said, mustering a weak grin. "Didn't think I'd see you so soon."

"Good to see you, too, David."

Her brother looked rough. His blonde hair was long and unkempt, and he had the beginnings of a scraggly beard. His orange jumpsuit was wrinkled, and his eyes looked tired. He had slimmed down significantly since the trial, and she was worried that he couldn't make it much longer.

"You look like hell," Maeve said, leaning back in her seat.

David chuckled. "Thanks, sis. You always know how to make me feel good."

"How are you holding up?"

David let out a deep breath. "Been better. But I'm hanging in there."

Maeve nodded, not sure what to say. She was worried for him. She had always tried to be there for her twin brother, but it was hard to know how to help him when he constantly made the wrong choices. If he had stayed away from his friends in the wrong crowd, then maybe he wouldn't have gotten this conviction in the first place.

"How's Mom?" David asked, in a hesitant voice, like he didn't want to hear the answer.

Maeve hesitated. For the second time that day, she had to be the bearer of bad news.

"Not good, David. She's getting worse."

Their mother's diagnosis had only happened since the sentence, and because she was so sick, she hadn't been able to visit. The last time Maeve spoke to her mother on the phone, she could only talk about how guilty she felt that she couldn't be there for David. She had asked Maeve to go see him as soon as she came into town.

"I guess a brain tumor will do that to you," he said.

Sitting across from her brother, Maeve was struck by the difference between the two of them. Even for fraternal twins, they had always looked different. Where she had olive skin, chestnut hair, and light brown eyes, he was the opposite - towheaded with bright blue eyes.

She was the natural rule follower, methodical and rigid. She had always been fascinated by her father's work, wanting to follow in his footsteps to put bad guys away.

David had been more drawn to the people that their father caught.

He was the free spirit.

He always wanted to spend his days playing outside, making concoctions in the sandy dirt. He used to secretly buy fireworks and set them off in abandoned parking lots, after spray painting random words onto the sides of buildings. As they grew up, this turned to selling cigarettes and alcohol to minors, and by the time they graduated high school, he had racked up a list of misdemeanors and petty crimes as long as his arm.

No matter what she did, Maeve couldn't convince him to get his act together. She knew her brother better than anyone, and because of that she knew he had a good heart. He was just lost.

But they all were.

Even Maeve felt unmoored, in her own way.

Different as they were, there would always be an understanding between them, a bond stronger than anything. After all, they had grown up under the same strict, unfeeling father.

"What if she goes...and I'm still trapped in here?" he said, still worried about their mother. His voice through the phone turned to almost a whisper.

Maeve felt a lump form in her throat at the desperation in his voice. She knew that he had never been able to come to terms with their mother's illness, and the thought of not being able to say goodbye to her was tearing him apart.

"I'll do everything I can to make sure you're there," Maeve said firmly, knowing deep down she was almost powerless to help him. Even still, her new job at the field office had to be worth something. Maybe she could ask her new boss to talk to the D.A.

"But you need to start making better choices, David. You can't keep going down this path."

David nodded, his eyes downcast. "I know. I've been trying to get my act together, but it's hard here. You don't know what it's like."

Maeve sighed.

She did know more than he realized.

With every arrest she made, she thought about her brother, and how the prison system had set his life on a course that was all but impossible to recover from.

She had seen how the system worked from the inside, and it was a vicious cycle that was hard to break. Even once he did get out, she knew he would struggle to get a job or find friends that weren't also ex-convicts. But she couldn't let him use that as an excuse anymore.

"I know it's hard, but you can't give up. You have to keep trying," she said firmly. She wished she could reach through the plexiglass and give him a hug.

"I need you to do something for me, Maeve," he said, his blue eyes pleading with her.

"Anything," she replied without hesitation.

"I need you to talk to Dad. He's the only one who can help me get out of here. If he puts in a good word with the D.A's office, maybe I can get my sentence—"

“I already tried that,” Maeve admitted, cutting him off before he could finish his request.

David's face fell, and Maeve felt a pang of guilt. Her brother had counted on her for help, and she had failed him.

“I tried as hard as I could, but you know how he is,” she said.

“Makes sense,” he said. "Do you remember that time I asked him to come visit school for career day, and he told us that he'd visit our school once our grades were out of the toilet?"

Maeve let herself laugh at the somewhat traumatic memory. Her father was nothing if not consistent.

"Weren't we in second grade?" she remembered.

"Or what about the time he told me, 'cops have more important things to do than attending shitty, half-rate theater productions of Peter Pan.' When we were ten."

"I forgot about that," said Maeve.

David shook his head as they reminisced about the childhood they shared.

“I can’t even get him to visit Mom. After all our family has been through, he won’t leave that garbage-dump of a trailer that he lives in.”

"I bet he'll come around. He always did eventually. You always were the favorite child, after all."

"No," she said, not wanting to finish the thought. *That was Veronica.* She almost said it out loud, but caught herself. None of them could bring themselves to say her name.

She instinctively knew they were both thinking about Veronica.

Maeve nodded, feeling the weight of their childhood memories settling over them. Their father's strict and unyielding nature had shaped their upbringing in ways that were hard to forget and Veronica's absence had left a hole in their family.

"I know it hasn't always been easy," said David. "I was there too. I remember what it was like."

She wanted to say something else about it, to finally say Veronica’s name, but then her phone rang in her pocket. The name of her new supervisor at the field office appeared on her screen.

"What do they want?" said David.

"I'm not supposed to start until tomorrow," she said with confusion on her face.

Maeve hesitated for a moment before answering the call. "Hello?"

"Agent Sharp." She recognized the voice as that of her new commanding officer. "We need you to come in right away," his voice sounded tense. "We've got a situation, and we need all hands on deck."

Maeve felt a jolt of adrenaline rush through her body at the urgency in his voice. "What's going on?"

"A body's been found in one of the casinos on the strip. It's... well... it's the owner's daughter. Top priority. I hate to ask you to do this, but can you come in today?"

"Of course," she said. And hung up the phone. "Sorry, bro. I'll visit as soon as I can."

"Leaving already, sis?" David asked, looking downcast.

Maeve hesitated. She hadn't even been able to be there for him during his trial, and now she was leaving again. Maybe she should reconsider. After all, who else did David have to really talk to?

"Don't worry about it," he said, as if reading her mind. "I'm not going anywhere."

He managed a grim smile and then looked down at the handcuffs around his wrists.

"I'll be back as soon as I can," she said. "And I'll ask about getting in touch with the D.A. I'll do everything I can to get you out of here. I promise."

"Thanks. I know it means you're sticking your neck out for me."

"That's what family's for."

As she drove to the field office to report for duty, the memories of Veronica weighed heavy on her mind. It was a part of her past that she rarely let herself think about, a secret she kept. Returning home threatened to unearth all the unresolved feelings that she had left behind.

But Maeve had a job to do.

If there was a killer on the loose, then Maeve had to catch him before other people got hurt.

She would bury herself in work, until the painful memories went away.

CHAPTER THREE

Maeve's route took her past the old familiar sights of Las Vegas. Where most of the world only knew this city by its casinos and nightclubs, Maeve knew the place was far more complicated than that.

She drove through the residential side of the city, where people's front laws were covered in palm trees, rock gardens, and cacti. She drove down the road where her old high school was, and found that it hadn't changed at all. The outside wall was still covered in the same huge mural of a lizard. She even drove past the park where she and her siblings had played, and she could almost hear their laughter as she looked at the empty swing sets and slides. She almost passed her mother's house, where her mom stayed all the time now, confined by her illness.

With her local knowledge of backroads that Maeve thought she had forgotten, she arrived at the FBI's field office quickly. It was late afternoon, and the sun was already dipping low in the sky.

She got out of her car once again, with a feeling of dread collecting in her stomach.

So far, the day had been nothing like she hoped.

One reunion after another had turned sour. Now that she was going into the office, it could only get worse. She was used to the high-profile cases of Quantico, where the best detectives in the world raced to find the most skilled killers. But Maeve had no idea what to expect from a regional field office, dealing with the cases of only one city.

She reminded herself to take a breath, and then walked briskly through the entrance, her heart pounding with a mixture of anxiety and dread.

Inside the building, the air was tense. Before Maeve could make it to the reception desk, a tall man dressed in a polo shirt, khakis, and loafers approached her. He had deep brown skin, and his black hair was cut short and neat, starting to turn gray at his temples. She recognized him as Agent Nathanial Williams from a brief video call they had weeks before, as part of Maeve's final interview.

"Agent Sharp," he said, with a polite smile. He reintroduced himself and offered her a firm handshake. "I'll be your supervisor here in the field office. I'm sorry that we're not meeting in person under more cheerful circumstances."

Maeve shrugged. "Detectives rarely met each other under cheerful circumstances at all."

"Even still. Welcome back to Las Vegas," he said.

Maeve gave him a polite nod. "It's strange to be back," she admitted.

"I believe it," he said passively, but Maeve knew that he knew very little about her background.

Maeve followed him past the entrance towards the back offices. "Thank you again for coming in a day early. This case… I'm sorry to say it's a little unusual for most of our detectives. LVMPD called us in for assistance this morning." Behind his exterior show of politeness, she could sense an intensity to him, with the way that he rushed through the halls.

"I'm afraid the official tour will have to wait," he said. "But I'll point out a few things before we get to the briefing room."

"Wait, Agent Williams, what's going on?" Maeve asked, trying to keep her voice steady. "What is so different about this case? Why bring me in early?"

"Well, technically you don't have to take this case if you don't want to. But in a city like this, most of the crime centers around drug overdoses, petty theft, attempted robbery. People trying to steal their money back from the casinos, or complications with loan sharks."

"But?" Maeve asked.

"To be honest, we don't get a ton of murders. And this isn't just a murder case. This victim was connected to some of the most powerful and rich people, not just in the city, but in the whole country. Her family is untouchable."

Maeve nodded, as she began to understand the shock of the victim's death. A high-profile family always complicated police proceedings.

As they walked, Maeve could sense an energy and anxiety in the air. She could hear the collective buzzing in the room, murmurs and chatter of other agents and detectives. Their shoes clacked over the linoleum floors. Williams pointed out their "copy room," which was a closet with an outdated printer that had an out of order sign taped on it. He pointed towards the interrogation rooms, and then he showed her to her desk. It was an old wood-laminate thing, tucked into the corner, stained with coffee-rings of the last resident.

Maeve made a mental note to do a little cleaning as soon as she had the chance.

Her desk was completed with an outdated Dell desktop and a rolling chair with a broken wheel. It didn't matter. Hopefully, she wouldn't be spending much time at her desk. Instead, she'd be out in the field, investigating cases.

Then Williams opened the door into the briefing room. The room itself was similar to the rest of the building: the brown wallpaper was peeling at the corners and the room was suffused with the shine of fluorescent lights. All of it was a far cry from the sleek, modern offices in Quantico.

The space had been converted into a place to investigate the new murder. A few reporters stood in the corner, asking agents to speak into tape recorders. Uniformed officers from the police precinct brought boxes of records. Everyone in the room looked up at her as she entered.

"Everyone," announced Williams to the room. "This is Agent Maeve Sharp; she just transferred from headquarters, so I want you all to give her a warm welcome."

Maeve scanned the room of stressed faces, fifteen people compiling all known information on the victim, her family, and her friends. A few of them offered a half-hearted hello before turning back to their work. These people were clearly preoccupied with an investigation that overwhelmed them.

"So what can you tell me about the case so far?" she asked.

"Our victim is Juliette Cavendish," Williams explained. "Her family was old money before old money was a term. Her dad, Kirk Cavendish owns a few places on the strip, but his most successful is *The Azure* , the most lucrative casino and resort on the strip. And because of that, Juliette had been rubbing shoulders with actors, musicians, Vegas socialites, anyone who drops big money on the casino floor, her whole life."

Williams walked Maeve to a wall full of pictures of Juliette. Some of them were taken by the paparazzi, showing her leaving expensive events or high-end restaurants.

"Her body was found by the hotel manager about 47 hours ago," said one of the uniformed officers. "LVMPD couldn't find any leads, so Mr. Cavendish demanded her case be handed to the feds." Maeve could hear bitterness in his voice– turf wars between local officers and federal agents could get a little complicated.

"The man's breathing down our necks about this one," Williams said with a frustrated sigh. "Making all kinds of threats about funding and support."

Maeve looked at Juliette as she had been while alive, smiling in a photoshoot for a magazine, with her honey-blonde hair perfectly styled over her shoulders, her glowing smile and perfect alabaster skin.

And then Maeve looked at the photos of the scene of the crime.

Each picture captured a different angle of one horrific scene. Juliette was lying on the bed in a baby-blue silk robe. Her hair was a matted mess, and her makeup ran down her face, as though she had been crying. Her skin was pale, her eyes shut, her lips parted. But most disturbing were the blackish-blue bruises around her neck.

Maeve felt a twinge of sadness at the sight of it. She had tried to harden herself to things like this, but seeing the horror of a new crime scene never ended. She took a deep breath, steeling herself for what was ahead.

"Cause of death was asphyxiation," explained Williams. "The coroner found nylon fibers in the skin— the killer could have used some kind of nylon cord or strap to do the job. Most of our detectives have gotten nowhere all morning," Williams said. "I know you don't start until tomorrow. And we can find you a simpler case for your first few weeks. But to be honest with you, we're a bit stumped by this one. Your experience in the field is going to be invaluable."

Even as Williams explained the situation, the brutality of this murder, Maeve still thought of her mother waiting in hospice care.

Maeve was supposed to spend the remainder of her ever-worsening day with her, listening to old stories about their family, back when they had all been happy.

"So, what will it be, Agent Sharp? Will you take the case?" Williams asked.

Maeve thought about it.

She knew that if she agreed, she would step into full swing in her new job, rather than the slowed pace she had hoped for when she transferred. Spending extended time with her mother and dedicating every spare minute to helping her brother get out of jail– her whole reason for moving here– would have to wait.

But she also knew that they couldn't solve this case without her.

A high-profile case like this was the chance to prove to her father that she was the detective that he had always pushed her to be, a chance to show him what she could do. It was an opportunity she had been waiting for, for a long time.

"I'll take it," she said, her voice steady and resolute. But even as she said it, she felt a sinking feeling in her stomach. Accepting the case would mean long hours, hard work. And just like the other detectives in the room, Maeve had no idea where to begin.

"Great. I'll introduce you to your partner," Williams said.

"What?"

"It's a good think you transferred in. No one has really been able to... uh... keep up with Jordan."

Maeve turned her head. What did that mean?

She could tell by the mischievous glimmer in Williams's eye that he knew something about this detective that she didn't.

"You didn't think you'd be working this case alone, did you?"

"No," Maeve said, knowing that she couldn't get so lucky. "I guess not."

CHAPTER FOUR

Williams led her down another poorly lit hall to a back office. They passed her new desk and the makeshift copy room on the way.

"He might not be the humblest guy on the squad," Williams explained, "but no one else solves cases like him."

Maeve's heart sank even more. She knew exactly what that meant— this new partner was a hot-shot detective that was hard to work with.

Sure, she hadn't exactly been known for always getting along with her partners in Quantico. She had a reputation for rushing through cases, getting results at all costs, but at least she didn't have a reputation for being outright cocky.

She followed Williams to the back of the bullpen, where her new partner waited, sitting at his over-cluttered desk, staring at his computer screen.

"Detective Eric Jordan, this is Agent Maeve Sharp," Williams said.

Jordan looked her up and down suspiciously before he stood up and offered her a half-hearted handshake. "Nice to meet you," he said, clearing his throat.

He was tall with a lean build, stubble shaded his sharp jawline, and he wore square glasses with heavy black frames, which gave him an intelligent but pretentious look. His dark wavy hair fell over his forehead in a messy swoop. He wore a suit that was slightly disheveled, in an "I woke up like this" sort of way.

"Eric will be invaluable on this case. He knows the strip like the back of his hand."

Maeve's heart sank even more at the description "Best detective we have here," confirming that her suspicions were true.

He looked up at Maeve, as though he could assess her abilities as an investigator with a single glance. He leaned back casually in his swivel chair.

"I've read your file. That McKelsky case you took care of in Virginia?"

Maeve smiled, flattered that he had read up on her previous cases. That case had been one of the toughest she had ever worked, where a serial killer had manipulated his victims into joining a cult. After months of hard work and long hours, Maeve finally caught the guy with enough evidence to put him away forever.

"You could have caught him sooner if you had realized that the print on the knife was a partial of the brother's...you know, in the Lorraine case, there was something similar, but it was really quite prosaic, once you think about it."

Maeve's jaw almost dropped.

She couldn't believe what she was hearing. Of course, weeks after the case closed, she had thought of this careless mistake herself, but no one else had ever pointed it out to her.

"Agent Jordan, please be polite to Sharp."

"The system didn't register the partial as belonging to anyone else," Maeve said, surprised that she was already defending herself to this man.

"Yeah, but that guy's file? His connection to that summer camp? Come on. I would have fingerprinted him right away."

Maeve felt her face turn hot with anger. She crossed her arms. "But I–" she was about to explain that she would have had to ask for the fingerprints, to match them to the crime scene, something that could have spooked him as a witness.

"*Jordan*," said Williams in a chiding tone, "Agent Sharp isn't some reporter you can impress. And she'll be taking the lead on the Cavendish case."

"But she just transferred," he protested.

Williams flashed him a look that told Maeve the two of them had discussed this kind of behavior before. "She just transferred from Quantico. She's solved dozens of cases like this one."

"Come on, I'm the best detective you have."

"Wrong." said Williams, with a satisfied smile. "You *were* the best detective I have."

Maeve couldn't help but smile too. She was enjoying her front row seat to the office drama unfolding in front of her.

"We agreed that you were lucky to not get a short suspension after what happened with your last partner."

Jordan huffed but didn't protest anymore. "Okay. At least she knows what she's doing."

"They don't let just anyone work at headquarters. She was on the fast track to the behavioral analysis unit, too."

"Is that so?" said Jordan, looking at her. A silent question hung between them. *So then what brought you here?*

But Maeve had dealt with her fair share of hot-shot detectives, and working with another one didn't intimidate her. She was ambitious too, and like anyone working for the FBI, she was anxious to prove that she could outsmart anyone else in the room. But something about the way Jordan talked took things a little too far. She wanted to know what he had done to get on Williams's bad side.

As to whether or not he was as clever as he thought he was, only time could tell. But Maeve had her doubts.

"Let's get moving," Maeve said. "We need to get to the crime scene yesterday."

Jordan stood and grabbed his jacket from the back of his chair. Williams handed her a file, stuffed full of paper.

"This summarizes everything we have on the case. There's a lot of ground to cover, so let's get started."

"Have you read up on the case yet?" Jordan asked.

"Well--"

"Maeve just agreed to come in early. This is a last minute case, and she's one of the few in our office who has extended experience with homicide investigation."

"Well, you can read on the way," said Jordan. "We've got to get to the strip."

***

Maeve was fighting motion sickness as she read the casefile from the passenger seat of a moving car. Jordan drove like he was in the middle of a car chase, with lots of jolting stops and starts. Maeve did her best to focus on the file in front of her and learn all she could about Juliette. She was splashed across the cover of tabloids on a regular basis, the subject of gossip columns, tweets, and Instagram posts. Her social media alone had millions of followers and a blue checkmark.

Several of the articles speculated about her relationship to the men that she had been spotted with by the paparazzi. Others accused her of drug abuse, repeated plastic surgery, and living off nepotism. But none of them stated anything conclusive about the real her, the kind of person that she actually was under all of the glamor and wealth.

Maeve looked over at Jordan, who kept his eyes focused on the road, uninterested in whatever she was thinking.

Maeve decided that if the two of them were going to get a long, she would have to extend some kind of olive branch.

"I grew up in Summerlin. My dad was a detective with the LVMPD," she began since he clearly wasn't going to ask. "Are you from around here?"

"I grew up here, too. Never left." His words were intentionally vague. Maeve wondered what he was hiding, but then again, her answer had been vague too. But Maeve knew that they didn't have to trust each other to work together.

"Sounds like you had a good gig in Quantico. What are you doing back here?" he asked.

This was the question that Maeve had known was coming. She pursed her lips, not sure what to say.

"Let's just call it family issues."

Jordan shrugged. "If you say so."

"So, what happened to your last partner?" Maeve asked. She knew that he would answer coldly, but she was so curious to know what happened.

"We didn't see eye to eye," he said. "He opted for an early retirement."

"Hmm." Maeve folded her arms. She might not know what happened now, but she'd figure it out eventually.

"I don't know about you, but I'm not here to be liked," he added.

"It can come in handy though," she added.

"You sound just like Williams," he muttered, but she thought she saw the beginning of a smirk come over his face.

By the time they made it to the strip, night had fallen. The whole street was illuminated with flashing lights, advertising gambling, shows, wrestling matches, and everything in between. The place had rightfully earned the nickname "America's Playground." The lights and signs attracted tourists, lured them in like moths to a bonfire.

As Maeve gazed out at the Las Vegas strip, she couldn't help but feel a complicated concoction of emotions. The flashing lights of the city were like a siren's call, beckoning people from all over the world to come and try their luck. But Maeve knew that behind the glitz and glamor lay a darker reality. The strip was designed to bewilder and blind, to distract people from the truth. The Luxor and NYNY stood tall and proud, their mirrored black glass pyramids sleek and imposing against the sky.

To one side of the road, a jungle of fountains danced with colored lights and gurgling water, forming a river of moving color, sparkling with the flash of cameras. It was like a dream world, a place where anything was possible. On the other side of the road, the millions of lights from hotels and casinos glittered and danced, hiding the desperation and heartache of those who had lost everything. Maeve watched as people crowded the streets, men wearing expensive suits and women in sequin-covered mini-dresses. They all laughed and smiled, but she knew that for most of them, the laughter was just a mask.

The clubs and casinos promised riches beyond their wildest dreams, but Maeve knew the truth. Luck was fickle, and the vast majority of people who came to this city hoping for a break would leave empty-handed.

As she watched their smiling faces, she couldn't help but wonder if Veronica had been one of those people, drawn to the strip by the promise of a better life, only to be consumed by the darkness that lurked beneath the surface.

The Las Vegas strip was a place of contradictions, a place that welcomed everyone and everything, and yet it had a darker, seedier side that lurked just below its glimmering surface. Despite the bright neon lights that illuminated the sky, there was a palpable sense of danger that permeated the air. It was a place where the rich and famous came to play, but also where desperate people made desperate choices.

The flyers for escorts and strippers littering the streets were a constant reminder of the darker side of the strip. The flashing lights hid a world of drugs, theft, and trafficking, where unsuspecting visitors were lured into dangerous situations.

It was a place that had claimed her father's life, his obsession with cleaning up the strip, along with the disappearance of his daughter, ultimately leading to his downfall. But Veronica was just one of many who fell prey to the trap.

As Maeve got out of the car and walked through the crowded streets, she couldn't shake the feeling of dread that settled in the pit of her stomach.

"Are you okay?" Jordan asked, noting her change of mood.

"Let's just get this over with," said Maeve. "We need to see that hotel room."

CHAPTER FIVE

As they pulled up to the entrance of *The Azure Heights Grand Resort*, Maeve was struck by the sheer grandiosity of the place. The building stood tall and imposing, a monolithic brick and marble palace. Pillars and statues adorned the exterior, crafted from materials like Roman glass, jade, and gold. White marble and rose-red stone shimmered and glimmered in the light, casting a rainbow of colors across the facade.

As they stepped inside, Maeve was disoriented by the dizzying spectacle before her. The hotel had been meticulously crafted to resemble Italy's timeless city. The flashing lights of the slot machines were overwhelming, casting a strobing glare that seemed to flicker in every direction.

The floor was covered in plush, ruby-red carpet, and the ceiling stretched high above, a dark, starless night. Maeve felt as though she had stepped into another world entirely, one where reality was distorted and skewed by the glittering chaos of the casino floor. The space was a veritable warehouse of light and sound, dozens of slot machines clashing together in a symphony of bells, sirens, and metal on metal. The noise was deafening, threatening to swallow Maeve whole in its overwhelming cacophony.

Juliette's tragic and untimely death had not even paused the flow of money in and out of the casino. People stood in a long line, waiting to receive chips in exchange for stacks of cash. They crowded around felt-topped tables, throwing dice, and thumbing through playing cards.

Servers rushed past, carrying platters covered in fancy drinks that Maeve couldn't even begin to name. Only the two security guards seemed to notice as the two detectives walked through the entryway into the main lobby.

"Last I heard, the local police are still securing the scene," said Maeve. "We should start there."

"What about the hotel manager?" said Jordan. "He's the one who found the body."

Maeve reluctantly nodded, angry at herself for forgetting this important step. She decided it was all because of the stressful day that she had been having, the overwhelming feeling of returning to this place after so many years.

But Jordan just gave a smug smile.

They made their way to the front desk, where they asked to be shown the correct place to go.

The concierge took them from the front of the hotel to the back offices. Inside one, the hotel manager was sitting at his desk, with pictures of sandy beaches on all the walls around him.

He looked up at them with an annoyed look on his face. "Can I help you? We're a little busy today."

"I'm Agent Maeve Sharp, and this is Agent Eric Jordan. We're both with the FBI field office, and we're here to assist with the Juliette Cavendish case." She placed her hands on her hips, trying to look authoritative even if she didn't feel it.

The man eyed them both skeptically. His nametag read "Richard Hart."

His bald head was shining with sweat, and his uniform was wrinkled, his tie askew. He had a roll of flab around his waist, and his pants were tight around his thighs. The lighting in his office was dim, but his face was lit by a desk lamp. He had a square jaw and a scar above his lip. His nose was crooked and one eye drooped slightly, giving a solemn, asymmetrical look.

He pushed up his glasses and turned away from the computer screen on the corner of his desk. He looked nervous to be speaking with them, and he wiped sweat off his forehead. "Of course. Anything for the feds. What do you need?"

"Can you tell us more about the crime scene? Walk us through what happened," Maeve said, getting straight to the point.

"I'll do you one better. I'll take you there myself."

He stood up and led them back into the maze of looping hallway corridors, designed to trap guests into staying in the hotel and gambling all their money away. Maeve followed eagerly behind. She hoped that she could find clues to this otherwise confounding circumstance.

"She had been staying in the penthouse for three months," said Richard. "Before that, she was on some find-yourself trip in Italy. Mr. Cavendish didn't really care what she did, though. No, his little girl always got what she wanted. He only allowed me to throw her out when the complaints became too much to ignore."

Maeve detected a hint of annoyance at the mention of Juliette.

"Did you interact with Juliette much?" she asked.

“Me? No, I don’t think she knew that I existed. But I did field every single complaint. First it was the noise. And then it was the trash. And then it was her guests harassing the rest of my staff.” He nervously looked back at them as he walked.

Maeve gave Jordan a sidelong look, wondering if his anxious demeanor meant he was guilty of something.

“Can you think of anyone who would have wanted to hurt her?” Jordan asked, a hint of irony in his voice.

“Well, I wasn’t always her biggest fan myself, to be honest. But I would never actually… well, you know. Besides, anyone famous has got to have enemies. You know, your stalkers and the like,” Richard explained.

Maeve frowned. "Any signs of forced entry?"

“You’ll have to ask the police what they found. I had to use a backup card to get into the door when I found her.”

The three of them stepped into a side elevator, and Richard pressed the button to take them to the top floor.

Jordan looked over at Maeve, a flicker in his eye. Even if he was proving annoying so far, there was something attractive about the way his blue eyes glinted. This whole crime scene seemed too clean. She wondered if he was thinking the same thing.

Juliette had been hiding something.

They were going to find out what it was.

As they walked down another long hallway, Richard became more forward about how difficult Juliette had been.

“She let a snake— a python— into this hotel! I helped hide it from her father but, I’ll admit, when Mr. Cavendish finally gave me the go ahead to kick her out, I was excited that I wouldn’t have to put up with her anymore.”

“Can you tell us more about what happened when you found her?” Maeve asked. “Any detail that stands out to you at all?”

“I noticed that room was a pigsty,” Richard returned. “At first when she didn’t open the door, I thought it was just her sleeping off a hangover. She did that a lot.”

Richard paused when they came to the penthouse door.

“Look, that night… I was working. I just want that…on the record.” He cut his hand through the air, as if he was trying to cut some invisible divide between them.

“We’ll get someone to check your alibi,” said Maeve. “And we’ll call you if we need more information,”

He breathed a sigh of relief. “I guess that’s all you can ask for,” he replied, and then he left them alone at the door.

Maeve decided not to suspect him at the present moment. He wouldn’t have offered up an alibi that wasn’t true.

As they stepped into the penthouse, Maeve took careful note of everything around them. The whole suite was nicer than any house that Maeve had ever lived in, and it was far roomier than her current living situation.

The first of its many rooms was filled with plush couches, each one upholstered with velvet. A luxury wool rug covered the floor, and the windows looked out onto the Vegas skyline.

After taking in the main room, Maeve stepped into the bathroom, where a clawfoot tub sat under another window. There was a rain shower big enough to sleep in, and a double vanity. Juliette had left it a mess, with high-end make-up spilled across one counter, and a bottle of perfume open on another, with towels littered all over the marble floor.

Maeve opened another door and found a walk-in closet full of designer dresses, evening gowns, and over a hundred pairs of high heels, some still in their original boxes.

Maeve’s throat tightened when she finally brought herself to look at the bedroom, where Juliette’s body had been found. The bed was unmade, and the silk sheets were rumpled, sliding to the floor. A cool breeze fluttered the gold curtains from the open window. More of Juliette’s clothes were thrown across the room, along with a few half-empty bottles of champagne, lipstick-stained wine glasses, and jeweled handbags.

Officers wandered around the room, taking pictures of the placement of everything and searching for DNA and fingerprints that didn’t belong to Juliette.

One of the officers appeared next to her, looking bored. He had his dark hair gelled back, and his badge read “Greg Laribee.”

“We’ve turned the place upside down, and haven’t found anything,” he informed her. “We’re going to release the crime scene to the feds now, but there isn’t much more to see. Everything that could be useful is already in evidence.”

“Nothing?” Maeve asked. “Look at this place, there has to be some DNA, fingerprints?”

"When I spoke with LVMPD, I was told that forensics is still processing it,” Jordan said. “But the place is full of partials, hairs, skin cells. She threw so many parties, it’s impossible to tell what could have been left behind by the killer or just another guest.” He turned to the officer. “You sure have a lot of security cameras. What about surveillance?"

Greg shook his head. "She requested that the cameras on this floor be turned off, so that no one could see her comings and goings."

"Security allowed that?" Jordan raised an eyebrow.

"She's the owner's daughter,” Greg said with a shrug. “What were they going to do? Risk losing their jobs?"

Maeve felt frustrated, but tried not to let the state of the crime scene get her down. She took the whole scene in, trying to commit it all to memory. She imagined the exact placement of the body as she had seen it in the crime scene photos. Even though she had been moved, she could still see Juliette’s imprint on the fine silk sheets.

Juliette had lived a life of such luxury, but none of that money had been able to protect her.

“I want to talk to everyone who had access to this room,” Jordan began. “Get me a list of the hotel’s entire staff.”

"Not so fast," said Greg. "You've got someone else to talk to first."

"Who?" Maeve said.

"Mr. Kirk Cavendish," he replied, with a sigh that couldn't mean anything good. "Well... let's just say I'm glad I don't have to talk to him. I'd get to that if I were you. He’s not exactly known for his generosity or understanding. The owner doesn't like to be kept waiting."

CHAPTER SIX

A few moments later, an assistant led Maeve and Jordan to the office on the first floor of the building.

“Who does this guy think he is,” Jordan muttered to Maeve under his breath. “The king of 17th century France?”

“Be quiet,” she said, hoping that the assistant didn’t hear.

The woman opened the door to the office, and Maeve's senses were immediately overwhelmed. Jordan’s instincts were right…the room was a dizzying display of wealth and extravagance, and Maeve had to resist the urge to gape in awe. The walls were adorned with an eclectic mix of art, from traditional oil paintings to avant-garde sculptures that looked like they belonged in a modern art museum. Maeve couldn't help but feel a bit disoriented by the jarring clash of styles.

The Persian rug beneath her feet was plush and soft, and the faint scent of bourbon filled the air. Maeve's eyes were drawn to the wall of windows, which offered a breathtaking view of the glittering Las Vegas strip below. The lights were so bright they seemed to dance before her eyes like a kaleidoscope of colors.

The furniture in the room was just as opulent as the rest of the decor. The plush silk chairs and sofa looked like they had never been sat in, and the dark hardwood floors gleamed as if polished to perfection. Ridiculous as it was, Maeve wondered what it would be like to be important enough to have an office like this.

As Maeve looked around, she noticed a large tank along one wall, filled with exotic fish she couldn't even name. The colors of the fish were so vibrant they seemed to glow in the dim light of the room.

As Maeve took it all in, she couldn't help but wonder about Mr. Cavendish. This office was clearly a statement to all his guests. It announced that he could afford anything, no matter the practicality, price range, or aesthetic.

"Finally," Mr. Cavendish said, leaning back in his leather desk chair.

Maeve stole a look at Jordan out of the corner of her eye, just to check that they were seeing the same out-of-this-world room, which was almost too much to take in at once.

He flashed her a barely noticeable grimace back.

Cavendish himself was short, with a rounded belly that made him look somewhat like an egg. His hair wasn't receding as much as most men his age, but it was gray as dishwater, with white flecks at his temples. He had a red face and round nose, and eyes that were sinking behind his wrinkled eyelids.

He wore an expensive suit that looked to Maeve like it could cost more than her car. To top it all off, he wore a purple paisley tie and a western belt buckle carved with a scene of a cowboy and a horse.

"Now, which one of you two numbskull detectives wants to tell me how you let this happen to my daughter?" he barked.

Maeve took a deep breath, and reminded herself not to raise an eyebrow or snap back with some smart-ass remark. She had met many rich and entitled people in her years as a detective, but something about Mr. Cavendish made her skin crawl.

He wasn't just rich and entitled. He had the attitude of someone who had been given everything they ever wanted since the day he was born.

"We're doing everything we can to find the person responsible for your daughter's death, Mr. Cavendish," Maeve said, keeping her tone level.

"Well, you're not doing it fast enough," he sneered, leaning forward in his chair. "Juliette was part of the establishment, and more than that, I don't enjoy having things taken from me. And now she's gone."

Maeve gritted her teeth, feeling her blood pressure rise. "We understand the gravity of this situation, Mr. Cavendish. That's why we're here."

"I want to know every detail of your investigation," he demanded, tapping his manicured fingers on his desk. "I want an email update every hour on the hour. I want to know who you've talked to, who you suspect, and what evidence you've found."

Maeve exchanged another quick glance with Jordan before speaking.

"We're still in the early stages of the investigation, Mr. Cavendish. We're exploring all possible leads and gathering evidence as we go."

"And we have to keep all information strictly confidential, should a conflict of interest arise," Jordan added.

Maeve nudged him in the arm. That wasn't the kind of detail that would pacify the man.

"Well, you better hurry up," he spat. "I'll have my team of lawyers on you if this isn't dealt with quickly."

Now Maeve understood why Greg had been afraid of this man. He had the kind of money that made his opinions and suggestions to law enforcement hold a lot of sway. There was an air of confidence about him that told Maeve that Cavendish knew how to play the game of politics and wealth; he knew how to gain control and get people to give him what he wanted.

"Do you know what a murder investigation could do to an establishment like mine?" he asked.

But Maeve guessed this meant he hadn't stepped outside of his office in the last several hours, where people crowded the casino floor as much as ever.

"I've paid off the newspapers to keep the story from breaking," he explained. "Those dummies on the casino floor can't look up from their cards for long enough to see the whole goddamn police department walk in. But once the news breaks, things will be different. When word gets around, the reputation of this hotel could be ruined. Ruined! I've spent years garnering favor from the high-rollers, and now look what has happened. We'll never get that good reputation back. *Never*."

Mr. Cavendish gave a small grimace, and reached into his desk for a cigar. He offered one to Jordan, who shook his head. Maeve felt a tinge of resentment towards this man... His daughter—his only child—had just been brutally murdered, and all he cared about were profit margins? He should be grieving instead of trying to force the investigation to move along at break-neck pace for his own benefit.

Maeve's job forced her to wonder what would happen if she turned up dead. After all, Maeve had a callous, cold-hearted father of her own, who would probably have similar priorities in the same situation.

"I'm going to cut straight to the chase," he said. "I read online that most murder cases are solved in 72 hours. I want this one shut in 48. And since her body was found yesterday morning, you're already over 24 hours behind. You'll find the bastard who took my Juliette from me. Am I understood?"

"I promise that we're doing everything we can to find the person responsible for your daughter's death, Mr. Cavendish," Maeve said again, refusing to make any promise about how long it could take to solve the case.

The man turned to face her, his eyes filled with an indescribable mix of anger, sadness, and despair.

"You better," he said, his tone laced with bitterness. "I worked my life to build all of this, and for what? So that my daughter can be taken like this?"

Suddenly, he was struggling to hold back tears. Maeve was confused at this sudden change.

As he looked out of the window, Maeve took a moment to survey the room. She knew that he was right— what was the point of all this wealth and power if it couldn't protect the ones he loved?

She thought back to an article she had skimmed as part of her research about Juliette's troubled relationship with her father. The girl had been open about her struggles with her father's distant and cold demeanor, and his tendency to try and fix things with money instead of love. Maeve couldn't help but feel a twinge of sadness for the girl, who had clearly never felt the warmth of a true connection with her father.

"I thought I had more time," he said. "To make it up to her. To deal with it. When she was a kid… you always think they'll grow out of it. That's what everyone says. The partying will get old, and they'll mellow out. I just thought we'd have more time. But now we don't. This is my last chance, the only way I can make it up to her."

Mr. Cavendish's confession lingered in the air, weighing heavily on Maeve's heart. In spite of herself, she felt pity for him. The pain in his eyes was palpable, a mixture of regret, desperation, and grief. She watched him take another puff of his cigar, his hand shaking slightly, before he spoke again.

"You have to understand," he continued, "I didn't know how to be a father. I never had one myself. All I knew was how to make money, and I thought that was enough. But it wasn't. I was never there for her when she needed me, and now it's too late."

Maeve listened silently, her mind racing with conflicting emotions. She couldn't deny the sincerity in Mr. Cavendish's voice, nor the pain in his eyes. It was clear that he was struggling to come to terms with his daughter's death, and that he was desperate to make amends for his past mistakes.

"I'm sorry," he said suddenly, turning to face Maeve and Jordan. "I know this isn't what you're here for. You're here to catch her killer, and I promise to do everything in my power to help you. But I just needed to say this. To someone who might understand."

"We'll find who did this," Maeve found herself saying. But as soon as she did she regretted it.

She was in no place to make such promises.

They had no leads, no evidence, no real information on the private life of Juliette.

"Good," he said, leaning back in his chair. "And I have one more thing to say. If you need any resources, anything at all, just let me know. Consider it done."

Maeve resisted the urge to roll her eyes. Just like that, any remorse or reflection was gone. Kirk the father was replaced with Kirk the hotel owner, the man with enough money to buy his way out of any problem that he could encounter. Rich people like him loved to throw their money around. That kind of bribery might work with other detectives, but it wouldn't work with Maeve.

Mr. Cavendish's eyes flicked to Jordan, and Maeve could see he was starting to get angry too. He had been strangely silent for their whole conversation.

"I don't think you understand the severity of this situation," he said, his voice rising. "My daughter was killed in a room in *my* hotel. This reflects poorly on me, and I don't tolerate failure."

Maeve could feel her own anger starting to escalate, but she knew she had to keep a clear head. "We understand, Mr. Cavendish. And we're doing everything in our power to solve this case as quickly as possible. But we can't make any promises about how long it will take."

He snorted. "I suppose I understand that. But I certainly hope you do everything in your power to solve this soon. Because if you don't, I'll make sure you both regret it."

CHAPTER SEVEN

Maeve and Jordan continued down the hallway, passing oblivious guests who were blissfully unaware of the danger that lurked in their midst. Maeve couldn't help but think about Mr. Cavendish and what it would be like to grow up with a father like him.

Sure, Maeve had her own problems with her father, but the man she just met was such a strange mix of pressure, anger, and regret. It must have been hard for Juliette, to be his one and only daughter, living under the constant pressure of the limelight.

"Can he really do what he implied?" she asked Jordan. "Can he get us thrown off the case?"

"When dealing with Kirk Cavendish, that's the least of our worries," he said. "He is wildly connected. He knows people in the mayor's office, the DA, even the director of the FBI field office. Williams's boss."

Mr. Cavendish's connections must have affected Juliette. Any problem she had could be magically erased— as long as her father stepped in.

But Maeve didn't have time to turn a police investigation into some political game.

"Let's just work the case like any other," she said. "I'm not going to let him intimidate me."

Jordan nodded. "The man has too much influence as is."

As they returned to the crime scene, Maeve looked around anxiously at all the people milling around the hotel, wondering if any of them were related to Juliette or her killer.

The unease only continued as she stepped into the room. Cleaners with the hotel were already stripping the bed and vacuuming the carpets. It was strange to think that after such a terrible event, the hotel would release the room to be rented like any other. In almost no time, the space had been converted from an active crime scene back into a high-end suite for the enjoyment of the Las Vegas elite.

The room was dimly lit, the only source of light coming from the flickering neon sign outside of the window. The whole space smelled like cleaning supplies and fingerprinting dust.

Maeve introduced herself to the last forensic detective in the room, and asked him what they found. He was tall and skinny, and wore a name badge that read "Stanley."

"We've been examining the room since the body was found," he said. "Our officers took samples back to the lab for identification purposes. After a thorough examination, we concluded that there were traces of DNA from multiple people in the room. Whether or not their presence was related to the crime was impossible to tell based on the information we currently have. It seemed that Ms. Cavendish's room was a regular host to large parties, making it difficult to determine what was part of the criminal activity and what was simply residue left behind after one too many late night gatherings."

"Thank you for your help," Maeve said.

"This is our last piece of evidence," Stanley said, and he handed her another evidence bag. Inside it was a designer handbag, glittering from behind the translucent plastic. "You can take it now. The rest of the items will be sent to the field office as soon as we process it."

The two detectives put on latex gloves, and Jordan took the purse from the evidence bag to examine it.

Maeve picked up the handbag, carefully examining it as she turned it over in her hands. The suede material felt smooth from the other side of the latex, but as she looked closer, she noticed faint scratches etched into the leather. It was clear that the bag had been well-loved and frequently used, which Maeve hadn't expected of a girl who could afford a new bag each week. The deep wine-colored handle caught her attention, with its bold gold accents that had dulled over time.

She shifted her attention to the gold clasp, which appeared to have lost its luster and was now tarnished. Maeve ran her fingers over it, feeling the roughness of the metal. As she opened the bag, the inside lining revealed a soft shade of purple, contrasting with the suede exterior. A small gold sachet from the casino's shop lay nestled in one corner.

The scent of lavender and rose perfume wafted up from the bag, reminding Maeve of the woman who had carried it. It was as though she had just sprayed the perfume moments before leaving the room. But the fragrance was not overwhelming; it was subtle, hinting at the woman's taste for simple elegance.

Maeve gingerly reached into the suede designer bag, her fingers brushing against the soft material before she found what she was looking for. As she pulled out the contents, she couldn't help but notice the weight of the bag and the gentle creaking sound of the leather against the zipper.

As expected, it contained several credit cards with the name "Juliette Cavendish" embossed in gold lettering. There were also a few crumpled receipts from high-end department stores and luxury bars, and celebrity restaurants.

But then her attention was drawn to something unexpected. A small volume of Wordsworth's poetry sat nestled in the bottom of the bag. The spine was worn and creased, indicating that it had been well-loved and read many times over. Maeve couldn't help but wonder what kind of person Juliette was.

A lover of luxury and fine things, yes, but also a reader of poetry?

Beneath all the fame, Juliette had an inner life.

Maeve was still convinced that Juliette had been hiding something before her death. Why else keep the security cameras off? Maybe this could be the missing piece that told her what it was.

As she gently turned the pages, she saw notes scribbled in the margins, indicating that Juliette had taken the time to truly engage with the text. Maeve felt a sudden pang of sadness. This young woman had so much potential, so much to live for.

Maeve carefully examined more of the book. She knew that this clue could be significant in solving the case. It provided a glimpse into Juliette's personality, her likes and dislikes.

"They found a copy of Moby Dick on her nightstand too," said Jordan. "This girl… she's hard to pin down. One minute you think she's just another spoiled kid, the next…" he trailed off as Maeve opened the volume of poetry and a few hundred dollar bills fell out.

"Whatever she was, she was ready to run," she said. "She must have had some enemies, or else we wouldn't be here."

"Can't argue with that logic. If only we had the phone unlocked."

"Maybe we can still check her social media."

Maeve took out her phone and searched Juliette's name on social media.

Most of the posts were typical— selfies and photos of her expensive outfits and vacations, with vague, emoji-filled captions, yet Maeve couldn't help but notice the occasional post that hinted at a darker side to Juliette's life. Some of the captions were photos of darkened windows, with short phrases referencing loneliness and isolation. One of them even read, "when there's no one else you can trust."

One post stood out in particular: a photo of Juliette with a man and the caption "Dangerous Liaisons." Maeve couldn't see the man's face, but she could tell that he was tall and muscular, with short dark hair.

"What do you think?" Jordan asked, peering over her shoulder.

"I'm not sure," Maeve admitted. "But it's something. We need to find out who this man is and if he had anything to do with Juliette's death."

"Did you try Googling him?"

"He isn't tagged. We need to talk to people who knew Juliette and might be able to identify this man. Maybe one of the bars, from the receipts in her bag?"

"Good idea."

***

After checking four bars and two clubs, the two detectives arrived at the last lead they had.

In the dark of night, the club's strobe lighting and heavy bass caused Maeve's temples to throb. The pounding beat rattled her mind, muffling all thoughts. Crowds of people danced in the flashing lights, yelling over the music, and spilling drinks.

The two detectives approached the bar, where one of the waitresses was mixing a neon-colored cocktail.

"We're with the FBI!" Maeve announced, yelling to be heard over the music.

The bartender looked up, slightly startled, but didn't give them the same cold glare that the others had. She was a petite redhead with freckles, dressed in black jeans and a white shirt. She was about 25 and had a tattoo of a red heart on her forearm.

"Do you know Juliette Cavendish?" Maeve asked.

The girl gave a slight chuckle. "Yeah, I'd say so. She's a regular here. She likes to bring her friends, and sometimes she buys a round for the whole place. Not so bad, as far as the customers we get around here go. What's going on? Is she in some kind of trouble?"

"Juliette was found dead yesterday morning," Maeve admitted.

The waitress covered her mouth with her hand and took a step back. "Are you sure? I just saw her, maybe last week at the latest."

"Can you think of anyone who might have wanted to hurt her?" asked Jordan.

The waitress shook her head, her eyes turned glassy. “I don’t know what to say. I mean, I guess I didn’t really know that much about her, at the end of the day. If you don’t mind me asking, how did she pass?”

“I’m afraid that detail hasn’t been released to the public yet,” Maeve answered. “Can you think of anyone who would have wanted to cause her harm?”

The waitress bit her lip and placed the drink mixer on the bar. “I know not everyone always got along with her. She had a bit of a strong personality. She had to, with a father like hers. But I can’t think why anyone would want to kill her. Unless it was for her money. She was pretty loose with it; it was like she had an infinite supply.”

“What about this man,” Maeve said, pulling up the photo from Instagram. “Do you recognize him?”

"That's Max," she said.

“Were the two dating?”

“It depended on the day. I saw them fighting several times, but they always seemed to make up. She never told me what about, even after I asked. He works at the bar on the top floor of the hotel across the street. If you hurry, you can probably stop him before his shift is over.”

“Shift?” Maeve said, giving Jordan a surprised glance. Juliette was involved with someone with a real job, not another trust fund baby?

“I never liked Max. He always rubbed me the wrong way. He skimped on tips too.”

“Thank you for your help,” said Jordan, offering the bartender his card, along with a wink and the invitation to call with more info.

“What do you think?” he asked, once they were crossing the street to go to the bar she mentioned.

“Constant arguing? It sounds like a motive to me,” Maeve said. “Let’s just hope he doesn’t see us coming.”

CHAPTER EIGHT

As they approached the hotel, Maeve could hear the thumping of music coming from the rooftop bar. The streets below were filled with people walking and talking, but up on the rooftop was a different story. There was a party atmosphere as people drank, danced, and enjoyed the view of fountains and pyramids that glowed in the night sky.

The terrace was lined with tables draped in white tablecloths and adorned with flickering candlelight. In one corner of the terrace there was a DJ playing music while people danced around him. At another table there were people enjoying drinks while they looked out on the beautiful scenery below them.

At one end of the terrace, there was a bar that stretched across the whole expanse. There were colorful cocktails lined up along its length, all lit up by neon lights behind them, making them appear to glow like magical potions atop their smooth surfaces. Behind these drinks, bartenders mixed more concoctions for customers to enjoy while they chatted animatedly among themselves.

At the center of it all stood Max, just as he was in the picture. He was flipping bottles in midair with an effortless finesse that commanded attention, even from across the room. His movements were graceful and mesmerizing— a combination of power, technique, and confidence that betrayed his true level of skill.

He was attractive, with tousled dark hair and deep brown eyes, but he moved a bit differently than the other club-goers; he was more solitary, more mysterious. Even though he flashed a smile at the guests, he wasn't a part of any of the social circles here.

Max continued to work his magic at the bar, juggling bottles, serving drinks, and impressing everyone who watched. He caught glimpses of Maeve every now and then as she and Jordan scoped out the place from the corner.

After they had watched for long enough, Maeve and Jordan approached the bar, both hiding their badges at first.

"Max Lorrimer?" they asked, using the name that the waitress had given them.

"That's me," he said, not looking up from a bottle of liquor that he threw in a graceful arc through the air. with another hand, he slid a martini across the bar to a girl in a backless dress.

"We'd like to ask you a few questions about Juliette Cavendish," Jordan said.

Maeve frowned. She thought that maybe Jordan was showing their hand a little too quickly in the effort to save time. If what the bartender said about this guy was true, then he was likely to be resistant to any questioning.

Max froze, and the bottle crashed to the ground, scattering broken class and alcohol all over the floor. He looked back at the two detectives, for a long, still moment. His face went white with fear. He looked from Maeve to Jordan, as if wondering which one would be harder to outrun. Then, he suddenly leapt over the bar and ran away in the opposite direction.

He charged out the doors, and even though Maeve and Jordan ran after him as fast as they could to the elevators, the doors closed just as they got there.

Maeve darted across the hall to the stairwell. "Come on," she urged Jordan, beckoning him over.

"We're on the twentieth floor, Maeve."

"And we'll beat him to the first floor this way," she replied. "It's like he did us a favor."

Jordan grimaced, and then followed her down the winding stairs, story after story. "Maybe we could repay the favor and wait for the elevator," said Jordan, running out of breath.

The two of them finally emerged on the first floor, and they rounded the corner just in front of the elevator, just as the door slid open.

"Going somewhere?" Jordan said between gasps, as Max appeared on the other side.

Maeve was too out of breath to say anything at all.

But he pushed past the two of them, out into the hotel lobby. Maeve stumbled after him, but Jordan had somehow gotten a second wind, and he sprinted out the door, right on Max's heels.

Max flew out the door and into the street, dodging cars, pedestrians, and street performers as he went. He weaved through a casino lobby in a blur, nearly knocking over a group of gamblers in his haste. When he emerged on the other side, it was clear that he was headed for an alley not far away.

“Is this guy an ultramarathoner or something?” Jordan gasped, throwing his head back.

Maeve had a stitch in her side, but she refused to slow down. He was the closest thing to a lead that they had. She couldn’t lose him.

Every muscle in her body begged her to stop.

Her lungs ached.

But she forced herself to carry on.

Once inside the alleyway, Max increased his pace as he darted between dumpsters and around corners with ease. Maeve was sure that this would be the end; he couldn’t escape the alley’s dead end. But just as he was about to stop and raise his hands, he jumped and grabbed onto one of the fire escapes. He pulled himself up onto the platform and then jumped off on the far side, behind Maeve and Jordan.

Maeve couldn’t keep herself from cursing. Max’s speed and agility were extraordinary.

Without flinching, Jordan took off after Max, his jaw set, his eyes dark.

All his complaining vanished as he darted after him. It was a side to him that Maeve hadn’t seen before, one that she hadn’t known existed. Now she was the one who wanted to slow down, but he charged ahead, his feet hammering on the sidewalk.

Even at a distance she could tell that his breath was labored and sweat beaded at his forehead. He pushed forward with a newfound focus, a strange determination to catch Max before it was too late.

But then— just as Jordan was about to reach out and grab him— Max made a sharp turn around one last corner.

Jordan was running too fast to turn as sharply, and his momentum sent him flying out of control. He slipped on the pavement, and lost his footing, crashing into the ground in an undignified heap of arms and legs.

Maeve almost paused to help him up, but he waved her on. “Keep going,” he urged.

If Max Lorrimer got away, they might never see him again.

Maeve nodded and ran, even though Max was almost to the far side of the alley. She ignored the pounding in her chest and the ache of her feet.

Max had made one last turn into a dead-end alleyway. He frantically searched for an escape route, but couldn't find one. A high fence blocked the other side, and he desperately tried to climb it, but it was too tall. He lost his grip.

He fell with a crash, back to the dirty pavement.

Then he turned, just in time to see Maeve running towards him.

She could see it in his eyes— he was trapped and he knew it.

But that only made him more dangerous.

"Stop! FBI!" Maeve announced, raising her gun.

With no other choice, Max lifted his hands above his head.

"Max Lorrimer, you're under arrest," she panted.

Maeve's heart was pounding as she recited his Miranda rights and cuffed him. His gaped mouth opened as if he wanted to say something, but he remained silent. Maeve wondered if she had made the right decision, but she had to do something to get closer to the truth.

If this lead proved wrong, at best it was a terrible waste of time.

At worst, it opened the FBI up to a wrongful arrest lawsuit.

Not to mention Mr. Cavendish breathing down their necks. Even though she had wormed her way out of a 24-hour deadline, he wouldn't be happy to hear about any kind of delays.

But if Max wasn't hiding something, then why run?

Jordan stumbled into view, panting heavily, sweat trickling down his forehead, and his hands shaking slightly. Maeve could tell he had pushed himself to the limit trying to catch Max. She had never seen him look so disheveled before, and it almost worried her.

"Oh good," he gasped, trying to catch his breath. "We got him. I was just about to—"

But he trailed off, and bent over so that his hands rested on his knees, as he tried to regain his breath.

"I think you've met your match, dude," Max said, looking at Jordan with a smirk.

"What is that supposed to mean?" Jordan shot back, his eyes flashing with anger.

Maeve stepped in between them, holding up a hand to stop Jordan from doing anything rash.

"Ignore him," she said, her voice low and intense. "He's just trying to get under your skin."

Max chuckled, his eyes darting back and forth between Maeve and Jordan. "You two make quite the pair, don't you?" he said. "The tough cop and the wounded hero. I bet you think you're hot shit, don't you?"

Maeve gritted her teeth, feeling her anger rising. Max was pushing all the wrong buttons.

"We need to get him back to the field office," she said, her voice clipped and tense. "We have a lot of questions for you, Lorrimer. And I mean, a lot."

She motioned for Jordan to take Max away, and he nodded, still breathing heavily. As they loaded him into Jordan’s car, she couldn’t help but feel the slightest bit afraid.

Max was their best lead, and she wasn't about to let him slip through their fingers.

CHAPTER NINE

Maeve stifled a yawn as she looked at Lorrimer from the other side of a one-way window. Jordan stood next to her, both of them watching their only suspect stew in the interrogation room.

"Want to call it a night, and I'll take care of this?" Jordan said.

Maeve gave him a suspicious look. "And let you get the credit?" she said. "Never."

Jordan smiled back.

But in truth she couldn't remember the last time that she had a good night's sleep, and the time change was still catching up with her. She wondered if this part of the job was one reason that her dad had declined so much— the things you saw in the field as a detective could make it hard to get any real rest.

"I didn't even do anything." Max's voice came through the intercom. "I thought you were someone else, that's why I ran."

But Maeve had seen a thousand suspects like this, and she could tell that he was guilty of something. It was in the way that his eyes darted around the room, the way he tapped his foot incessantly.

There was an intensity to the room, a desperation.

A few of the other detectives poked their heads in to gawk at the new suspect.

Maeve wondered how she would handle the interrogation. Even though he was their strongest suspect, they still had little to go on.

Inside the interrogation room, the sterile, concrete walls were bare, save for a single clock ticking away in one corner and an American flag draped across another. A long wooden table occupied the center of the room, chairs on both sides that gave off an air of authority. A bright lamp hung from the ceiling above it, providing a sense of clarity to proceedings.

Maeve and Jordan watched him in silence for several moments.

"This was the right decision, right?"

Jordan shrugged. "It was a little risky. We can only hold him for a few hours without charging him, so we'll have to get the information we need quickly. If not, he walks free and we never learn what he knows."

Her last supervisor used to tell Maeve that she was too forceful in her techniques. That she didn't have the patience required of a good detective. But she got results that way, and her hunches had never led her astray.

"The only other option was just letting the guy run," she said.

Maeve crossed her arms and gave Max a closer look. He was fidgety, scared.

"Do you hear me?" Max yelled at the mirror. "I want a lawyer. I'm not saying anything without one."

"I hate it when they say that," she said.

"You hate due process?" Jordan joked.

"It doesn't exactly help us find the actual killer any faster."

"You don't think he's the actual killer?"

Maeve crossed her arms. "It makes sense, doesn't it? Angry ex. Maybe it was an accident."

Even as she said it, she wasn't completely convinced.

"Not to mention, we found a keycard to Juliette's hotel room on him. That's pretty strong evidence to me," Jordan added.

"We'll have to see what he says about that."

The two of them pushed through the heavy door and stepped into the room.

Max was visibly shaking, his eyes darting around the room as if looking for something to cling onto. The door slammed shut behind them. He started defending himself as soon as they entered, insisting that he didn't do anything, that this was a violation of his rights, that he would have them both thrown out of the FBI for this.

Nothing Maeve hadn't heard before.

But something about him still didn't add up. He was handsome, but not in Juliette's same rank.

Maeve and Jordan sat down at the table, where Max was waiting.

"I didn't do anything," he repeated.

Maeve leaned forward in her chair and looked him in the eye. "We just want to find the truth. Why don't you start by telling us how long you were seeing Juliette?"

Max's eyes widened in surprise. "What? I-I wasn't seeing her. We were just friends."

Maeve's gaze didn't waver. "Really? Because we found a key card to her hotel room in your possession. We know you were in her room."

Max's face paled. "Okay, fine. We had a thing. We were kind of on and off. Juliette, she's not the easiest to get along with. All that attention can only go to a person's head. But it's over now, okay? This time for good."

Maeve noted the use of present tense. The story of Juliette's death still hadn't broken in the mainstream news. She looked at Jordan and could tell that he had noticed the same thing.

Maeve raised an eyebrow.

"How did your relationship end?" Jordan asked.

Max frowned, retreated deeper into his seat. "Look, I wouldn't say it was amicable. Is that what you want me to say? She just drove me so crazy sometimes, with all her partying and drinking, like nothing was ever enough for her."

"Are you aware that she was found yesterday morning?" Maeve asked, and then she remembered the time. It was so late that it was already the next day. "Well, two mornings ago, I guess," she corrected herself.

"Dead?" His face went pale. "Is Juliette…shit…" He trailed off and ran a nervous hand through his hair. "I swear, I had no idea that she was dead. Are you sure it's her? I thought it was about the—" he froze.

He didn't seem to be too grieved to find out that his ex had been killed. He was just trying to cover his own skin, protect himself from any kind of trouble. He ran a frantic hand through his hair and drummed his fingers on the wooden table.

"Look, I didn't know. I didn't have anything to do with that. I saw her a week and a half ago. I went to her hotel. And I ended it, alright. She didn't… she didn't kill herself did she? Because if she did that…"

"Right now," said Maeve, "we're investigating a murder. We need to know any information you have."

"Look, the security cameras will— actually she said she turned those off. Shit. I don't know what else I can say."

"If you didn't kill her, can you think of who might have wanted to?" Maeve said, hoping that he would sputter, get desperate, and reveal something.

"I don't know. Why don't you ask her father? Or that damn hotel manager. He hated her more than anyone."

"If you didn't kill her, then why did you run?" asked Jordan.

He gave a heavy sigh. "Look, I just—" he nervously stammered, tapping his leg and fidgeting. "I was stealing from her, alright. Is that what you want to hear? I ran because I was stealing from her."

It was strange to see a man so intimidating, dark, and mysterious look so frightened.

"Stealing?" Maeve led.

Max sighed. "It started small at first. I'd take a little bit of cash here and there out of her purse before she came back to the room after dinner or shopping. It was stupid, I know, but I needed it more than she did." He paused, looking down at his hands as he wrung them together nervously.

"But then it got bigger and more frequent; I'd take jewelry too when she wasn't looking. I thought that if I took a little bit at a time, she wouldn't notice."

Max gave a remorseful sigh. "Look, I needed the money and she didn't, alright? I have loans, I have debts."

But Max's sudden candor only made Maeve more suspicious. If Juliette found out he was stealing her money, she could have threatened to tell the police. He could have killed her to cover his tracks.

Max shook his head. "I'm sorry. I don't know what else to say. She didn't have a lot of enemies. Not a lot of face-to face-enemies. But she didn't have a lot of friends either. It was hard to tell with her. She could be really distant sometimes. I'm sorry I can't help you more."

Maeve knew that there was nothing more that he could tell her.

"Can you tell us where you were, the night before tonight, between 10:00 PM and 1:00 AM?"

"Yeah," he said. "It's called The Desert Rose. Ask around, they'll tell you I was there."

"Just a moment, please," Maeve said, and she nodded to Jordan that it was time for them to leave the room.

As they walked out the door, she thought of the hundreds of dollars they found in the poetry book, and wondered if Juliette knew about Max's theft, but did nothing about it to keep him around. All details about her inner life showed a lonely girl, trying to mask her insecurity with drinking and buying love and affection.

"I don't believe him," Jordan said. "I think he's our guy. I think she found out he was stealing, and when she threatened to tell the police, he killed her."

Maeve sighed in frustration. "No, that can't be it," she said. "He had to have known that killing a famous socialite would only open him up to more investigation. He didn't even know she was dead. He used the present tense when referring to her."

"So? Maybe he's just a good liar."

"He was so agitated when he thought we brought him in for theft. He calmed down once he started telling the truth. I think we should release him, put a hold on his passport, and check his alibi."

"Release him? After what we went through to catch him? He's our prime suspect, and you want to send him out on the streets? Do you know what the journalists would say if they ever found out we let our only lead go?"

"I don't care about journalists!" Maeve snapped. She was just doing what was best for the case. She didn't care how other people would see it.

"Come on," said Jordan. "What about the key card?"

"There are a thousand other reasons that he could have a keycard, and any defense attorney worth the paper his degree is printed on will tell you that much. We have to at least check the alibi."

"He's just trying to run out the clock, send us to track to some fake alibi, and by the time we find it, he's gone. We arrest him now, and in a few days, there will be a photo of me in the paper shaking Kirk Cavendish's hand."

"I prefer to do investigative work *before* arresting someone."

Jordan rolled his eyes. "I thought you would be less of a stickler."

Instead of dignifying this with a response, Maeve turned on her heel and left.

She went into the briefing room to tell someone to get over to the nightclub, but of course, no one was there.

"You should call it a night, Maeve," Jordan said, catching up behind her.

She didn't want him to tell her what to do, but somewhere deep down, she knew he was right.

She was frazzled, tired, and frustrated with Jordan and his need to prove himself right all the time, though it reminded her of that same quality in herself.

I just need sleep, she thought.

Being back brought up a part of herself that she wasn't sure she was ready to face.

Living here was going to be harder than she anticipated.

"You only have 42 more hours to hold him," she said. "If that's what you really want to do." She grabbed her bag and searched her pockets for her car keys.

"Come on, Maeve. We'll get this guy," said Jordan.

"You keep saying that," Maeve said. "What make you so sure the killer is a man?"

CHAPTER TEN

As the woman walked through the strip at night, the neon lights illuminated her face, casting a glow on her porcelain skin. Her make-up was flawless, with smoky eyes that hinted at a bit of danger. A slash of red lipstick adorned her full lips, making them seem even more inviting. Her long, flowing hair was styled to perfection, cascading down her back in loose waves. Her glittering fingernails caught the light, sparkling like diamonds in the night.

Despite her striking appearance, no one around seemed to be paying her any attention.

She moved with purpose, her sequined dress shimmering in the light, as if she were on a mission.

She was hiding a secret that only she knew.

Her gaze darted around, taking in everything and everyone around her, as if searching for something or someone specific.

As she continued down the sidewalk, the click of her heels echoed through the empty street, the only sound to break the silence. It was as if the entire world had stopped to watch her.

But no one was looking for her.

What was she doing out here, alone in the middle of the night, and why was no one else paying any attention to her? The woman remained an enigmatic figure, leaving those who saw her with more questions than answers.

The people of the Vegas strip were shallow, she thought. It wasn't their fault.

They worked their meaningless desk jobs in blank, colorless cities, only so they could come here, to lose all their money to professional gamblers, or to overspend on fine hotels, to get roped into buying cocaine, only to barely make their flights back to their boring towns, to do the whole thing over again.

But they couldn't help it, could they?

She had never wanted that life.

She had never wanted to be ordinary, dull. Simplistic.

The noise of the strip faded into the background as she focused on the path in front of her. It was like the crowds of people weren't there at all; the street performances, the partiers, none of it mattered anymore. The only sound that registered in her ears was the clicking of her own heels on the pavement.

She approached one of the many hotels, this one the more economic option, for the tourists on a budget. Still, it was nice, with sixty well-lit stories stretching into the sky.

A thin smile crept across her lips.

Even though it wasn't a main attraction of the strip, the building made everything around it feel insignificant and small in comparison.

She stepped inside and found compensating decoration, made to feel like a high-end establishment. The walls were decorated with gold paint, the floor was a deep red carpet, and the chandeliers sparkled in the dim light. Not one hotel employee looked up as she passed through the lobby. Even if she didn't feel like she belonged there, she knew how to dress the part. She reminded herself that with a cocktail dress and red lipstick, no one would question why she was there.

Her outfit had been perfectly chosen to fit in.

She was almost invisible.

She stepped onto the elevator, and rode it to the fifteenth floor. When she stepped out again, into the hallway, she kept her face turned away from the one security camera guarding the hallway.

As she wandered further into the hotel, she could feel her heart racing. But she strengthened her resolve.

She finally arrived at the end of the hall, and knocked on one of the identical doors.

It was as if the hotel was holding its breath, waiting for her to make her next move.

When the door finally opened, she was greeted by a woman with jet black hair and piercing green eyes. The woman's gaze made her uneasy, but she managed to hold her composure.

Even though it wasn't a suite, the room behind was beautiful, with a classic style four-poster bed covered in a crisp white bedspread, a bright red armchair in the corner, and wallpaper decorated with flourishes of gold. A thick rug of woven silk draped across the floor, giving the room an air of elegance in the smaller space that it offered.

"Yeah? Can I help you?" said the room's owner, with a valley girl accent.

The sight of her made the guest ball her fists. She felt a surge of hatred well up in the back of her throat.

In the light, the woman standing before her was a vision of beauty: long chestnut hair cascading down her shoulders, perfect skin that had no blemishes or wrinkles, and mesmerizing eyes that shimmered in the dim light. Her body was slender and petite, but toned like an athlete with curves that were highlighted by her simple yet fashionable dress. She had a grace about her.

But the woman knew that she wouldn't be so beautiful for much longer.

Without saying a word, she quietly slipped through the door, drew a rope from its hiding place in the folds of her dress, and expertly wound it around the other woman's throat.

CHAPTER ELEVEN

The morning sun woke Maeve from her slumber, and she groggily opened her eyes. At first, she had no idea where she was. The bed was unfamiliar, the sheets were a different color, and the curtains were made of a strange fabric that she had never seen before. The room was strangely narrow, like one long hallway.

Then it all came back to her as she remembered the place she had chosen as her new home.

She had decided to take up residence in a mobile home like her father, but instead of an old, run down trailer, she had purchased a renovated RV, something she could drive around from place to place.

She had found a tiny trailer park in the middle of the desert, far away from all the hustle and bustle of everyday life. This was the only place she could afford, but it offered its own unique beauty.

The park was situated in a large circle with the other 5th wheels, campers, and RVs parked at least 20 feet apart from one another. The center of the circle was open with tall cacti covering it. Some of the plots housed trailers, each with a small porch made up of painted wood planks that wobbled slightly as you walked on them and strands of twinkling lights wrapped around railings and posts that lined the sides of walkways and stairs.

The sun shone brightly against the pale cream walls of Maeve's trailer home during the day, warming it up without the help of the heater.

She had used the last of her money to customize the RV herself. Its interior was modest but comfortable, with new appliances and big windows.

The walls and furniture were light colors, giving it a bright airy feeling that allowed Maeve to spread out her belongings and have ample storage space. A large living area included two plush armchairs and a giant sofa with soft, fluffy cushions that doubled as a pull-out bed.

Maeve took in the morning sun from the comfort of her home as she looked out at the desert while drinking her coffee and listening to the morning news on the radio.

While she listened to the quiet morning and watched the still desert, she couldn't help but miss the apartment in D.C.

Sure, it had been a drive to get to the FBI headquarters every day, but the view of the Lincoln memorial had been worth it.

The apartment itself had been spacious with clean white furniture and great views of the skyline. It had an air of elegance in the smaller space that it offered, and even though she no longer lived there, those times were still fond memories.

The furniture had been sparse but luxurious with white couches and a glass coffee table that reflected the sunlight streaming through the windows. The kitchen was small but efficient, and Maeve often cooked meals for her co-workers in that tiny space.

On clear nights, Maeve would turn off all the lights in her apartment and stand underneath them to look out over Washington, D.C.'s skyline. The cityscape always made her feel so small yet connected to something much bigger than herself. She would stand there for hours, just taking it all in until she felt like she was part of a greater world.

Maeve had loved living in D.C.

It was her own way of hiding from what happened to Veronica.

As Maeve stood outside, the early morning sun just starting to peek over the horizon, memories of her past flooded her mind. She could almost hear the sound of her sister's laughter and feel the warmth of her embrace. She could still hear her father opening the front door of her childhood home, coming back from working a case late into the night.

While Maeve and David's relationship was strained by the differences between them, she and Veronica had been inseparable, two peas in a pod, always finding ways to make each other laugh.

But then things changed. Their parents' divorce left them both shattered, and they were forced to split their time between their childhood home and their father's run-down apartment.

Thinking about those times now, Maeve wished she could go back and do things differently. She wished she could have been there for her sister more, and could have helped her through their parents' divorce. She had to remind herself that she had only been a kid too.

She wished she could have one more morning on the porch, sipping hot cocoa and watching the sunrise.

But she knew that was impossible. All she could do now was honor her sister's memory and try to be there for the rest of her family. It was her responsibility, and she took it seriously. So she took a deep breath and made her way inside.

The more she thought about it, the more she understood why her dad chose this kind of life. There was a simplicity to it that was almost a relief after thinking about complicated cases and the grief of other families all day.

She was angry with him for how he chose to respond to their family's tragedy. She was angry that when she lost her sister, in a way she lost her dad too.

Yet, despite the resentment she felt towards him, Maeve knew that she couldn't completely deny the similarities she shared with her father. She was strong-willed and determined, just like him. That was perhaps the reason why she had the courage to move away and start a new life, even though it meant leaving her family behind.

As she prepared for her next visit, Maeve couldn't help but feel the weight of responsibility on her shoulders. She was the only one left to take care of her family, now that her brother was in jail and her father was unwilling to leave his trailer. It was a heavy burden to bear, but Maeve knew that she had to be there for her mother, who was wasting away in their childhood home.

Despite the sadness and the pain that lay ahead, Maeve steeled herself for the visit. She knew that it wouldn't be easy, but someone had to be there for her mother. And so, with a deep breath and a heavy heart, Maeve set out to face the challenges that lay ahead.

She was the only thing keeping her family together— what was left of it at least.

Before she could get up to refill her coffee, her phone rang.

She answered and heard Jordan's voice on the other side. "Good morning, sleeping beauty," he said, with a relaxed, refreshed voice. "I hope you're well-rested."

Maeve didn't want to hear from him.

She knew that her response to his theory about Max had been somewhat of an overreaction, a result of her tired mind and built up frustration. She wasn't exactly known for being easy to work with.

But at the same time, she trusted her gut; it was her case, and he hadn't respected that. She didn't want to rehash it all now, in the quiet of the morning. She was hoping that they could get along well enough to keep working together. Even if Maeve was intense, and rushed around protocol, Eric Jordan was cocky and he had too much trust in his own perception.

"I got a full three hours in," Maeve said sarcastically, playing along for the sake of it. "You sound pretty rested yourself."

"Well that's good, because I'm not. Were you planning to come into work today, or should I just finish this case up without you?"

Maeve checked her watch. "Jordan, it's 7:00 AM."

"And yet, crime never sleeps." Then she heard him sigh on the other side. "Look…someone checked on Max Lorrimer's alibi. Someone confirmed he was at the nightclub at the time of death. You were…"

Maeve waited for him to say it.

"Right," he finally managed.

"I'm sorry, I didn't hear that," she teased.

"Too bad because I'm never saying it again. I was right too, I was just a little bit… less right."

"You sound so surprised," she said.

"I'm only surprised that guy has friends," he chuckled. "But your instincts were right. I released him as soon as I found out."

"I guess we're going to need a new lead."

"It's looking that way."

Maeve stood up and poured the rest of her coffee into a travel mug, feeling ready to continue with the case. "I'll be there in half an hour. Don't solve it without me."

"No promises."

CHAPTER TWELVE

Maeve arrived at the field office with a sigh, her messy bun and wrinkled clothes having been pulled from a moving box telling the story of how tired she was. She imagined that the dark circles under her eyes were visible to everyone in the room as she made her way over to where Jordan was sitting.

He was already on the phone, and he handed her a cup of coffee without looking up at her.

"I know, Mr. Cavendish," he said.

Maeve took a sip of the warm beverage. A soy latte. How had he known?

"That is how deadlines work, Mr. Cavendish," he reapplied.

Another moment where she heard the muffled sound of yelling on the other end of the call.

"Of course," Jordan finished, and then hung up the call.

"Same impossible deadline?" Maeve asked.

Jordan nodded. "It usually takes a month to solve a case like this. He wants us to know that we're almost late for our 24-hour deadline."

"Did he give a new one?"

"He said that if there isn't an arrest by the end of the week, there will be 'serious consequences.'" Jordan rolled his eyes.

Maeve took another sip of her coffee, already wondering how she would finish the case in time.

"Thanks for the coffee," she said, trying to change the subject away from Mr. Cavendish.

"See? I can be nice sometimes," he said with a smirk.

She gave him an appreciative look before setting down the cup and turning towards him expectantly.

Was this his attempt at a peace offering?

Nothing like this ever happened in Quantico. Maeve had dealt with her fair share of hot-shot detectives who wanted to take all the credit for cases, but none of them had ever tried to be friends.

He looked like he hadn't slept for a second. His clothes were rumpled and his eyes had dark circles underneath them too.

Even though they had just fought, Maeve couldn't help but feel a small pang of sympathy for him—he was obviously exhausted from working on this case all night.

Jordan looked up at her sheepishly, as if to say 'I'm sorry' without actually saying it.

"Look, I know I can ruffle feathers. But to me, the most important thing is that the case gets solved."

"Don't mention it. "Even if I was right," Maeve said jokingly.

"I'd call it a 'difference of vision,'" he retorted.

"So, did you find anything interesting while I was gone?"

Jordan swirled back in his chair, surprisingly casual as he opened the new case file on his desk.

"I checked all of Lorrimer's credit card statements. All his bank statements. It's clear that he was stealing from Juliette. I'll inform Mr. Cavendish. He'll probably press charges, but it's out of our hands now. I've also checked on all her most recent internet stalkers, and any death threats that she'd ever gotten."

"That sounds promising," said Maeve.

"Think again. Most of them were out of state, had an alibi, or aren't traceable."

Maeve sank into a chair across from Jordan and buried her head in her hands. "My first case here, a crushing deadline, and I can't find *one* promising lead."

"Hey, don't beat yourself up," Jordan said. "Even I can't figure it out, so that's when you know a case is *really* unsolvable."

"Ha-ha," she said flatly, slumping onto the desk. "I only risked everything in my life to come live here. Gave up my home. My friends."

"You had friends?" Jordan said.

"You're jokes are getting stale," said Maeve, knowing that this was his round-about attempt at cheering her up. "And they are not helping."

"Would it help if I told you that I got her bank statements, and it wasn't as much as I was expecting? I mean, it was a lot, but not like *a lot*, a lot. I think her dad must have kept her on a pretty tight leash. Well… relatively speaking."

"Still doesn't explain why she was the one found dead. Low funds is a motive for people *to* murder, not a reason that people *get* murdered."

"Fine," he muttered. "Just trying to spitball here."

Maeve looked up to find that he was giving her an encouraging smile despite the frustration that they both felt. Was he actually being kind and considerate? This was a new side of him that she didn't think existed.

"There's got to be something we've overlooked, some small detail that will crack this case wide open. We just have to keep searching, and eventually it will lead us to the guy."

Maeve nodded, determined to find out the truth. As she studied Jordan's face, she realized that her initial assumption about him had been wrong—he was a lot more than just a hot-shot detective.

He was someone who cared deeply about getting justice for Juliette and finding the person responsible for her death.

The two detectives spent several hours looking over all the information that had been gathered in the case thus far. They reviewed every detail once more, from Juliette's bank statements to any suspicious activity that had occurred near the various mansions, penthouses, and properties owned by the family in the past few weeks.

They also looked into any recent deaths with similar circumstances, though nothing turned up yet. Still, both of them held onto hope—hope that they would eventually find something that could help them break this case wide open and bring justice to Juliette's family.

Maeve felt an even greater sense of pity towards Juliette as they went through her personal effects together—photos of her smiling brightly, treasured books and notebooks filled with scribbled thoughts. A life so full of promise cut short due to a senseless act of violence—it just wasn't right. And Maeve knew she would do whatever it took to make sure whoever was responsible faced consequences for what they had done to this young woman.

All Juliette had wanted was true companionship, but people either used her for her money or dismissed her as a shallow and vain princess.

With no other direction to go, Maeve started reading more police reports, not knowing what she was looking for. Maybe this wasn't the first offense of whoever did this. She thumbed through page after page of police reports until she found something interesting.

It was a report from eight days ago of a woman named Emily Smith, who had been found dead in her hotel room.

The cause of death: asphyxiation.

Maeve stopped in her tracks when she read that.

She scanned through the details of the case and noticed that some strange clues were present— the coroner found traces of nylon in her skin, indicating that some sort of nylon rope had been used to kill her.

"Jordan, look at this!" Maeve said, trying not to get her hopes up.

"This woman was killed in the exact same way that Juliette was. It has to be related."

He scanned the file, reading the relevant details as fast as possible.

Maeve explained her thinking. "A woman of the same age range, found dead in her hotel room, no forced entry. It's exactly the same. Right down to the cause of death. They even found... get this... traces of nylon in her skin. It has to be the same person!"

Maeve shot out of her chair, spirits automatically lifted.

Jordan intently read the report, and nodded, realizing the implications of what Maeve was saying. His brow furrowed in concern as he asked why they hadn't noticed this before.

"I don't know," he said. "But it's a bit of a stretch. This woman is really different from Juliette. Not much of a pattern."

"Come on," she insisted. "The nylon? The exact same MO? It has to be connected, at the very least, if not the same perp."

"Why wasn't this brought up sooner?" Jordan asked. "We've been searching through police records all day."

"I don't know," Maeve admitted. She returned to looking at the report. Now that she gave it a closer review, she realized it was surprisingly short for a death of its kind.

"Look," she pointed to one statement on the coroner's report. "They're calling it an accidental death. How is that remotely accidental?"

"I mean…" began Jordan. "Do you want me to explain to you…"

"Come on. In what world could someone be fully asphyxiated by accident. It says that her larynx was completely crushed."

"But why would they report it that way?" Jordan asked. "It makes no sense."

Maeve bit her lip, stumped by the same problem. "What if…" she began with a half-formed thought. "The hotel is covering it up? You heard what Mr. Cavendish said about cases like this and what they could do to hotels."

"I'd buy it," Jordan agreed.

Maeve felt a sudden anger rising within her. Her hands balled into fists, she couldn't help but feel a sense of frustration.

This was an important investigation. High stakes, with lives on the line, and this hotel had tried to cover it up.

The thought of someone getting away with murder made her blood boil.

But Maeve knew that she couldn't let her emotions get the best of her. She needed to stay level-headed if she was going to uncover the truth.

It was bad enough that someone had gotten away with killing two women, but what angered her more was the careless treatment of the evidence, covering up the facts. Even if the hotel wanted to cover up the truth, Maeve knew she had to uncover it. Only then could she find justice for Juliette.

"I think we need to pay this hotel a little visit," Jordan said. There was a flash in his blue eyes that told her he shared her frustration.

"I think you're right," said Maeve. "This case doesn't just have one victim anymore."

CHAPTER THIRTEEN

As Jordan and Maeve made their way through the grand entrance of the hotel, they were immediately struck by a sense of foreboding. The expansive lobby, usually bustling with activity, was eerily quiet, the only sound the murmur of hushed voices.

The only movement came from a solitary bellhop, who looked up briefly as they passed but quickly averted his eyes. Maeve couldn't help but feel a sense of unease wash over her, as if she was walking into a trap. Every step they took towards the elevator seemed to amplify the tension in the air, and she could sense Jordan tensing up beside her. She tried to keep her breathing steady and her eyes focused ahead, but she couldn't shake the feeling that they were walking into something far more dangerous than they had anticipated.

As Jordan and Maeve approached the elegant reception desk, with its gleaming marble surface and polished brass fittings, they were greeted by a woman who seemed to exude an air of superiority. She was tall and slim, her posture erect, and her movements graceful. Her dark hair was swept back into a tight bun, accentuating her chiseled features and high cheekbones. Her eyes were a piercing blue, and her thin lips were painted a bright red, giving her an almost regal appearance.

Maeve could tell that the woman was not someone to be trifled with. There was a coldness in her eyes that made Maeve feel as though she was being judged, and a subtle hint of condescension in her voice as she addressed them. Her nametag was so shiny that Maeve almost couldn't make out the letters spelling her name: Jessica.

"Good afternoon, can I help you?" she said in a frosty tone.

Jordan cleared his throat and stepped forward. "Yes, we're here to investigate a case. The murder of a young woman in one of your hotel rooms."

Her expression turned cold, and she narrowed her eyes suspiciously. "I'm sorry, but there must be some mistake. There hasn't been any sort of incident reported here."

Maeve felt a knot of frustration building in her stomach. She knew that Emily's death wasn't an accident, but the woman at the desk seemed intent on denying that anything had happened at all.

"Ma'am, we have reason to believe that a young woman was found dead in one of your rooms. We're here to investigate and get to the bottom of what happened."

"I assure you," said Jessica, "there must be some confusion. What happened to Emily was a horrible accident, but it was no one's fault. Our staff followed all the proper procedures and protocols."

Jordan leaned in closer, his voice low and insistent. "We're not leaving until we see the room and gather some evidence. So either you can show us the way, or we'll have to find it ourselves."

After a tense moment, the woman finally relented, her lips pursed in disapproval.

"Very well," she said curtly. "I'll show you to the room in question. But I'm telling you now, what happened to that girl was a terrible tragedy, and nothing more."

As Maeve and Jordan followed her towards the elevator, Maeve couldn't help but feel a sense of unease. Jessica's words had been dismissive and cold, as if Emily's life didn't matter at all. But despite the woman's resistance, Maeve was determined to find out what really happened to Emily, no matter how much the hotel staff tried to deny it.

Maeve and Jordan stood outside the hotel room with bated breath, exchanging a knowing glance before Jessica finally unlocked the door.

As soon as they stepped inside, the stale smell of cleaning supplies hit them like a ton of bricks. The room was eerily quiet, except for the occasional hum of the air conditioning unit. Maeve's eyes scanned the room, taking in every detail. The bed was neatly made, and the furniture looked like it had been rearranged. It was clear that someone had tried to make the room look like nothing had ever happened there.

Jordan began questioning the woman about the room, but she seemed to dodge his questions with practiced ease. Maeve couldn't help but feel a knot form in her stomach.

"Why did you clean this room up?" Maeve demanded. "This was a crime scene. Tampering with this area is illegal."

"Like I said," Jessica chided. "I'm not aware of any crime scene here. The circumstances of Emily's death, though unfortunate, were inconclusive."

Maeve gave an angry sigh, and looked around the room anyway. Even though all traces of Emily had long been cleaned away, maybe she could find something in looking at the room itself—the shape, the placement of the bed, the view.

In cases like these, the scene of the murder was always chosen specifically. The killer had chosen this place to attack Emily, where she was the most at home, but also the most vulnerable.

"Can you tell us anything about Emily?" Maeve interjected, trying to redirect the conversation.

Jessica hesitated for a moment before finally answering, "She worked for us as an events coordinator."

Maeve and Jordan both frowned at this restrictive information.

"We do have a few of her personal belongings downstairs, if you'd like to see them?"

"Of course," Maeve answered, angry that this hadn't been a suggestion sooner.

Jessica showed the two detectives back down to the first floor and into a back office. A few cluttered desks were pushed against the windowless walls, painted lime green as if to give some illusion of being outside.

"Here you go." She handed Maeve an old cardboard box that had clearly been used to ship things before.

Maeve frowned. It was surprisingly light weight.

"Did she not have anyone come and get these for her?"

"We've tried contacting the sister," said Jessica. "But we haven't heard anything back from her."

As Maeve opened the box, a faint scent of lavender and something else, something metallic, hit her nose. She gingerly picked up Emily's phone, its screen cracked and shattered, with a few unread messages from an unknown number. She couldn't help but wonder who was trying to reach Emily, and what they wanted from her. A notepad was filled with illegible scribbles and drawings, but one page stood out— a list of names, with a few crossed out in red ink. Who were these people, and why were they important to Emily?

The earrings, dangling from a small velvet pouch, were simple yet elegant, with tiny diamonds glinting in the light. Maeve wondered if Emily wore them on the night of her murder, and if they held any clues.

She unfolded the clothes, noting the faded colors and frayed edges, wondering if they held any significance. The leather jacket, with its worn patches and scratches, seemed to tell a story of its own. And the tangled earbuds, with a few strands of brunette hair caught in them, made Maeve's heart ache with sadness. These were the only remnants of Emily's life, the only clues to her past, and yet they had little to tell about the person who owned them.

In a small way, Emily and Juliette were similar.

Both young women trying to make a way for themselves in the crowded nightlife of Vegas, with few people close to them, few they could really trust.

"I wonder if they knew each other," Maeve muttered.

"Who?" Jessica asked, but Maeve just gave a polite smile to decline the question.

Why did no one come looking for her, she wondered? That was one glaring difference—Mr. Cavendish practically had the whole Nevada FBI on this case, leaving no stone unturned.

But Emily's death was a silent one, and it had nearly gone unnoticed.

"Thank you," Maeve said.

She nodded and turned to leave. Jordan, however, stopped her.

"Excuse me," he said, "can you tell us anything else about Emily? Did she seem upset or troubled in any way?"

Maeve was impressed by his tenacity, especially with such a resistant woman.

Jessica hesitated for a moment before answering.

"Well," she said slowly, "I did notice that she seemed a bit on edge lately. I thought maybe it was because of the stress of planning the big show we had here last week, but now... well, now I don't know what to think."

Maeve and Jordan exchanged a knowing glance. Maybe others were suspicious about the circumstances of Emily's death. Maybe one of them had noticed something.

Still, if there was any eyewitness evidence, then why had no one come forward?

"Thank you for letting us know. We'll be sure to follow up on that."

Jessica nodded and left the room, leaving Maeve and Jordan alone with Emily's belongings.

Maeve picked up the phone and examined it closely. She wondered if there were any clues in Emily's call history or text messages that could shed light on her state of mind before her death. But so much of it felt like a dead end. Had Emily been chosen because she was so hard to trace? That theory didn't leave much room for Juliette…

Maeve had hoped that another victim would at least shed some light on the case. Provide new evidence. New clues.

But Maeve felt more lost than ever.

Jordan, meanwhile, was flipping through the notepad. "Looks like she was jotting down some ideas for the event," he said. "Nothing too revealing here. This girl didn't have much to her name," said Jordan. "I can't find anything on her. No police record, no other details."

"I know," said Maeve. "How long do you think it will take to get this phone open?"

"This isn't Virginia. It could take a week just to get the warrant. We're still struggling to get the service provider to help us out with Juliette's phone."

"And emergency contact on record for the hotel? If she was working here she would have had to..."

"I'll check," Jordan cut her off, storming out of the room and down the hall.

Maeve forced herself to take a breath, as she thought of Veronica once again. The guilt that she had long suppressed began to resurface, making it difficult for her to concentrate. She wondered if she had done enough to find her sister back then, and if there was anything she could do now to ensure that justice was served for Emily. Maeve was haunted by the past, and the present case was only making it worse.

Moments later, Jordan returned with a torn-off piece of legal paper.

“The phone number of the sister,” he said. “It was all they had on her.”

Maeve wondered why Emily was so hard to trace— almost like she was trying to hide, like she didn’t want to be found.

“We should go back to the field office,” Maeve said. “That’s a call I don’t want to make in public.”

CHAPTER FOURTEEN

Maeve sat at her desk, staring at the number on the piece of paper in front of her. Her heart was racing, and her palms were sweating. She knew she had to make the call, but the thought of it made her feel sick with anxiety. She had been in this situation before, making phone calls to family members of victims, and she knew it was never easy.

But this time was different. This time, Maeve was calling Emily's sister, and it felt more personal.

She remembered the call that she had gotten for Veronica.

"What are you waiting for?" Jordan asked.

Maeve didn't answer. She focused on what she had to do, rehearsing a thousand different versions of what she could say.

Maeve took a deep breath and closed her eyes, trying to calm her nerves. She knew that making the call was the right thing to do, and that finding out as much as possible about Emily and her life was crucial to the investigation. But still, she wished she could put the task off for another time. Finally, with a shaky hand, she picked up the phone and dialed the number.

The phone rang for what felt like an eternity before going to voicemail. Maeve took a deep breath and tried again, her heart racing as she waited for someone to pick up.

As the phone rang, Maeve's mind was racing with a million different questions. Who was this sister? Did she know anything about Emily's life? Could she provide any information about what happened to her?

"Hello?" said a confused voice on the other side.

The woman sounded hesitant, and Maeve could hear the sound of shuffling and a child crying in the background.

"My name is Agent Maeve Sharp, I'm an investigator with the FBI."

"FBI?" the woman on the other end answered. "What's going on?"

"I'm sorry to call with bad news," Maeve said slowly. "Is this Angela Smith?"

"Yes? What's this about?"

"Are you aware that your sister was recently found dead in her hotel room?" Maeve asked.

There was a long moment of silence.

“Yes, someone called me a few days ago,” she said. “Apparently it was a terrible accident. They were trying to get in touch with me for a while.”

“I am afraid the nature of your sister’s death has been called into question. You were told it was accidental, but we’re investigating it as a murder case.”

Maeve heard a sharp breath on the other side of the line, followed by a long pause.

Maeve knew exactly what it was like. She knew that Angela wouldn’t want to talk. If she was anything like Maeve, she would want to scream, to throw things, to kick walls. It was the only way that she knew how to respond to grief.

"But they told me— what really happened?" her voice shook, and Maeve could tell she was struggling to hold back tears.

"We're still trying to figure that out, but I was hoping you could help us. Do you know anything about what she was doing in Las Vegas?" Maeve asked, hoping to get some leads.

The sister hesitated for a moment before replying, "Emily didn't tell me much about her life there. We weren't very close."

Maeve shook her head, to let Jordan know that this was another dead end.

"What can I do?" Angela finally asked, her voice shaky and unsure. "I have to fly there, I have to--"

"We'll put you in touch with our field office," Maeve said. "They will give you all the information you need."

Angela's reluctant, shaky voice broke into all-out tears. "I can't believe...it’s just so... how did this happen? Why would the FBI be involved?"

Maeve did her best to calm Angela's racing thoughts. "We'll put you in touch with someone at our field office, they’ll give you any remaining details. Right now, all I can tell you is that the coroner's report suggests asphyxiation as the cause of death. We are investigating the evidence of foul play. Please don’t share this with anyone else, as it is sensitive information."

Maeve hated how cold and heartless her explanation sounded.

Angela wept silently on the other side.

Angela's voice cracked as she spoke. "We lost touch when she moved to Vegas. I should have done a better job keeping up with her."

"Ma'am, there's nothing you could have done," Maeve added, again knowing how little this would mean to someone who lost her sister.

"Do you have any idea who she might have been with?" Maeve pressed, hoping to get more information about Emily's recent activities.

Angela hesitated. "I don't really know anyone she was hanging out with lately," she said. "We haven't talked in a while, like I said."

Maeve had a sudden pang of guilt, remembering her own relationship with Veronica that had been strained at times. She wished for just one more chance to make things right. She could imagine the guilt and heartache that Angela was feeling.

"I'm sorry," Maeve said quietly. "This must be hard for you to accept."

Angela sniffled on the other end, trying desperately not to cry. "Yes," she said quietly.

Jordan elbowed Maeve, reminding her they had a job to do. Maeve didn't call to be a friend. She needed to know more about who Emily was. Only then could they find out why she died.

"Angela," Maeve said slowly. "I know this is hard. You can always reach out if you need anything, but we need to get back to work."

"Wait," she said. "Last I heard, she was working at some hotel for a famous singer who had a residency there. That's all I know. I'm so sorry. I don't think it's suspicious, at least I didn't at the time… It could be nothing."

"Thanks for the information. Please, don't hesitate to call if you think of anything else. We'll stay in touch and keep you posted if we find anything else."

When she hung up, Maeve looked over to Jordan and relayed the new information.

"Sounds like a new lead," he said. "Let's go."

***

The detectives' eyes felt heavy, their muscles ached, and their minds were clouded with exhaustion when they returned to the hotel where Emily had worked. The two had been working non-stop for hours, chasing leads and trying to piece together the puzzle of Emily's death. Yet, they pushed on, determined to find justice for the young woman.

But Maeve was still struggling to understand just how the two women were connected. Though they'd been the same age, there was little to indicate if they had known each other, gone to the same places, or had mutual friends.

The place had woken up since their last visit, now that it was later in the day. As they walked through the bustling casino, the noise of the slot machines and the chatter of the gamblers made it difficult to think. The flashing lights were disorienting, and the detectives felt a sense of unease as they navigated through the maze of tables and slot machines.

Despite their exhaustion, they approached every person they could find, asking if they knew anything about Emily or if they had seen anything suspicious. They felt like they were hitting a brick wall, until they finally found one of Emily's coworkers.

She was one of the waitresses at the bar, and she wore a long black dress as she carried drinks back and forth from the casino floor.

“What do you want to know about her?” she asked when they first caught her attention. “I thought that what happened was an accident.”

“No,” Maeve said. “We think that it is very likely that there was foul play. What else can you tell us about her?”

She was hesitant to speak with the detectives, clearly uncomfortable with the situation. She spoke in a low voice, looking around nervously as she answered their questions. The detectives couldn't help but feel frustrated and fatigued at the lack of progress they were making.

"Look, I'm sad for her, but it wasn't like I knew her well," she whispered, impatient to return to one of the tables. “I thought it was an accidental death anyway,” she added.

Maeve felt a twinge of anger push through her exhaustion. The two stepped away from the waitress and looked for someone else to talk to.

“Only an idiot would believe that a strangulation like that was accidental,” she said to Jordan.

“Okay,” Jordan said, putting his hand on her shoulder and guiding her away from the table. “We need to try a different approach.”

“These people aren’t even sad that their coworker is dead,” Maeve observed.

“You would think that they would be shocked. How often could something like this happen in a place like this?” Jordan said. “Then again, if operations pause for even one minute in a place like this, the employees can get in big trouble. The whole thing relies on the fact that the casino has been designed to draw people in and keep them there.”

Maeve looked at the dead-eyed gamblers in wrinkled suits, bachelor parties of frat-boys throwing bills down on the table, running their hands over the piles of red and black chips.

“I guess you’re right. We should talk to someone who isn’t on the clock.”

The two of them tracked down a female bartender, taking a cigarette break on the restaurant loading dock.

The two found a twenty-something girl, lines of stress etched in her forehead and the corners of her eyes. There was a lack of color in her skin, a dullness to her hair. She leaned against the wall, her eyes half-closed and hands in her pockets, blowing smoke down the alleyway. Her hair was wild, and curly, her clothes were wrinkled; she reeked of cheap, artificial vodka and cigarettes.

Pungent smoke floated from the bartender's cigarette, but still she took another long drag, inhaling deeply.

"I still have fifteen minutes on my break, if that's why you're here," she said in a callous, deep voice, mistaking them for other employees.

"Actually, we're here for something else," Maeve said, flashing her badge.

"Shit," the bartender said. "What did my little brother do this time that they sent the feds?"

"We're here in connection with Emily Smith, your coworker."

"Oh," said the bartender. "In that case, you can just forget I have a brother. Emily? Yeah, it was a huge shock. I’m still a little suspicious. Accidental death, are you kidding me? But you didn’t hear that from me.”

"What can you tell us about her?" said Jordan.

She shrugged. “She was pretty quiet. From out of town, came here to work in show-biz, or something like that. I don't really know. She kept to herself a lot. That events coordinator job title was bullshit. It just meant she was an extra waitress most of the time, running interference for the high rollers."

"Did she have a boyfriend?" Jordan pushed.

“Aren’t you coming out of the gate strong? Not that I know of. All I know is that Alexa loved her, and I mean *loved*. Couldn't get enough of the girl. promoted her so quickly, you'd think the rest of us were slacking off."

"You mean Alexa Kyle? The jazz singer?" Maeve said.

"Yeah," the girl responded. "She has a deal with the casino. She's doing shows here for a few months before she goes on tour with her new album."

"And she promoted Emily?"

"Almost immediately. Emily is her assistant. Or was, I guess. Emily wanted to go with her when she went on tour, but Alexa drew the line there. Emily said it was because Alexa was 'jealous.' I think it was just good business."

"Thank you for your time," said Jordan. He flashed her a half-hearted smirk as he leaned forward to hand her a crisp, white piece of paper from his pocket. "If you think of anything else, feel free to call me. Here's my card."

"I'll do that, detective," she returned, with a noticeable glimmer in her eye.

Maeve rolled her eyes, pretending she didn't notice any of it.

As they left the casino, Jordan pulled Maeve aside.

"I'm going to do you a favor and choose not to report that," Maeve teased.

"I was being helpful. The key to good police work is building rapport with the witnesses."

Maeve huffed.

"I didn't know the famous singer was Alexa Kyle," Jordan added.

"Impressive," Maeve remarked. Maeve recognized the name because the jazz singer's relaxing ballads were among her mother's favorite music. She had a few old CDs in the glove compartment of her car, and the rest of her albums downloaded on her phone.

"No, it's not that," Jordan said. "Alexa Kyle was a known friend of Juliette Cavendish."

Maeve's heart skipped a beat. "How did I miss that?"

"Well," mused Jordan, "not everyone can have a steel-trap mind like me."

Maeve rolled her eyes again. "Then we have to talk to her. She's the only person connected to both victims."

CHAPTER FIFTEEN

As Maeve and Jordan approached the stage, they could hear the faint sound of saxophone music being played in the background. As they got closer, they saw Alexa Kyle standing center stage, her body swaying rhythmically to the smooth jazz sounds emanating from the massive saxophone beside her.

The atmosphere was electric, the air thick with anticipation for the upcoming show. The red velvet curtains draped around the stage gave the impression of a grand theater, and the spotlights set to either side of the stage created a dazzling display of light and shadow. Maeve couldn't help but feel a sense of awe at the spectacle before her, and for a moment, she was transported to another world.

Listening to the familiar music brought back the few good memories she had.

She remembered going on long car rides with her mom and siblings through the desert, or sitting outside on Sunday afternoons. Alexa Kyle was one of the artists who was a staple of Maeve's childhood.

It was strange to meet her under such bizarre circumstances.

As Alexa continued to play, Maeve noticed the small details that made up the stage. The multi-colored bass drum stood in the corner, its vibrant hues almost glowing under the lights. The microphone on the stand gleamed in the spotlight, ready for use. The entire stage was a work of art, carefully crafted to create an unforgettable experience for the audience.

But even as Maeve admired the stage, she couldn't shake the feeling that something was off. The red curtain on one side of the stage hung precariously, as if it could fall at any moment. And there was a strange energy in the air, a sense of foreboding that Maeve couldn't quite put her finger on.

Alexa Kyle was the picture of elegance, standing confidently at center stage in a stunning white, form-fitting jumpsuit, and black boots added a touch of edginess to her outfit, while a red scarf wrapped snugly around her neck provided a pop of color. A black beret perched atop her head gave her an air of sophistication.

As Alexa began to sing, Maeve couldn't help but be drawn in by her beauty. Her face was perfectly sculpted, her lips forming a slight pout as she poured her heart and soul into the music. Her long brown hair cascaded in waves around her shoulders, framing her face like a halo.

The band behind her played with perfect synchronization, each instrument adding its own unique flavor to the mix. Alexa's voice soared above them all, filling the room with its beauty and power. Maeve was entranced, completely caught up in the magic of the moment.

Jordan continued to watch with an appreciative gaze as Maeve took a step closer to the stage, drawn in by the sound of Alexa's voice. It was a voice that commanded attention, rich and soulful, conveying emotions that Maeve could only imagine. She felt a shiver run down her spine as Alexa hit a high note and held it, her eyes closed in concentration.

As the song came to an end, Alexa looked up, surprised to see them standing there. Maeve could see the exhaustion in her eyes, the weariness that came with endless rehearsals and performances. But even so, Alexa's presence on the stage was electrifying, her passion and energy contagious.

"I'm sorry to interrupt," Maeve said, stepping forward. "We're with the FBI. We're investigating a case and we need to ask you a few questions."

“We’re in the middle of our rehearsal,” said Alexa, in a somber voice. “Whatever you have to say, it can wait.”

“Look, darling, I know that what you do is very important. But what I do is important too, and if I don’t get in my rehearsal time, then I won’t be able to perform my best. And a few big names are coming to tonight’s show. So why don’t you contact my manager, and maybe I can fit you in after a few weeks. M’kay?”

Maeve crossed her arms, unsure of how to proceed with a woman who refused to cooperate. She felt so deflated, knowing that this woman was the one whose CDs she had listened to for years. Never meet your heroes, as the adage went, turned out to be great advice.

“I’m sorry for the inconvenience,” said Jordan with the most disingenuous voice he could muster. “But unfortunately for you, FBI murder investigations take precedence over… what exactly is it that you do here?”

He was intentionally stoking Alexa’s anger, a small repayment for the way that she had treated them.

“If that doesn’t work for your schedule,” he added, “then maybe we could bring you down to the police station for refusal to cooperate and withholding evidence.”

"I'm sorry," Maeve said, "but it's important that we investigate all possible suspects."

"Suspects?" Alexa said suddenly. "Am I a suspect, detective?"

"We're not ruling out any possibilities," said Maeve.

She raised an eyebrow in response. "Are you threatening me detective? Do you know how insane you sound?"

Maeve took a step back, not wanting to intimidate a singer she had revered for so long.

"I have a team of lawyers that earn in a month what you make in a year. How do you think they'll respond to this?"

Maeve took a deep breath in, and let it out slowly. Her respect for Alexa was beginning to fade.

"Look," she said, after a few long moments of silence. "I don't know anything. I'm just… it's just…" her voice trailed off. "Just give me five minutes."

Moments later, she stepped off the stage and met the two detectives in a dark corner of the room.

"This better not be about what I think it's about," she complained.

"We're here to talk to you about the deaths of Juliette Cavendish and Emily Smith, both of whom were found strangled earlier this week," Maeve said.

She watched Alexa closely for her reaction. These had been two of her friends, but Alexa seemed to be ignoring the reality of their deaths.

Alexa's brow furrowed, and she leaned back against one of the walls.

"Yeah," she admitted, her voice taking on a darker tone. "I heard about that. Juliette and I were friends, from way back when she tried to trick me into getting her into show business. But the girl couldn't sing to save her life…" she looked up, realizing what she said. "Poor choice of words. That's not what I meant. I just meant…" she trailed off.

"What about Emily?" Jordan redirected.

Alexa seemed even more conflicted at the mention of her name. Her mouth twitched into a deep frown, and she tucked a lock of her brown hair back.

"She was the best assistant I'd ever had. And I'll miss her a great deal."

"When was the last time you saw either one of them?" Maeve asked.

But Alexa's open demeanor faded. "I don't know," she snapped. "You'll have to check my calendar. I don't keep that kind of information off the top of my head. I don't mean to get in your way or anything, but I have to prepare for my performance."

Maeve and Jordan exchanged glances. Acting so cagey was always suspicious. Could Alexa be hiding a motive that she had for killing both of them?

"Then I don't suppose you know what you were doing during the time of Emily's death eight days ago. Or two nights ago?" Maeve asked.

"I was probably performing," she said.

"Were you close with them? Juliette or Emily?" Maeve asked.

Alexa sighed. "You know how it is. Juliette, she just wanted attention. She was a little exhausting, to be honest. She was a lot closer to me than I was to her. It was like you could never listen enough; no matter what you told her, that you were her friend and you were there for her, she never believed you. She was just drowning in money. No matter how much she spent, she could always get more. She didn't understand that attracted the wrong kind of friends."

"And Emily?"

"She was the one who actually understood the business." Alexa looked off into the distance. "She wanted my job too, but she was the one who actually deserved it."

Maeve's ears pricked at this…Emily was gunning to become a successful singer, just like Alexa? Maybe a move like that could have displaced Alexa, threatening her position as one of the top performers in the city.

And by her own admission, she had found Juliette annoying. She could even be lying about not feeling threatened by her.

But even with the new information, Maeve got the sense that Alexa was a good liar— she was capable of spinning stories and making it all come out how she wanted it to.

"Do you have any idea who could have done this to them?" Maeve asked. She was far more interested in how Alexa responded than what she said. She watched Alexa's face closely for traces of guilt.

"I wish I did," she said, with slightly overblown sadness. She shook her head and scrubbed her eyes with her fingertips, smearing her mascara down her cheeks.

Suddenly, Alexa broke down into tears. Black, make-up-filled droplets of water streamed down her face. She sort of stumbled towards Maeve, and before she could back away, Alexa had wrapped her in a bear hug.

It was all Maeve could do not to shove Alexa off her. One moment, she was excited to meet one of her favorite musicians, the next disappointed that she turned out to be a pretentious jerk, the next they were hugging.

"I'm so sorry…" she sobbed onto Maeve's shoulder. "I've been trying to hold it together. The band needs to be strong. But Emily was like my sister. And Juliette…"

Maeve flashed Jordan a concerned look over Alexa's shoulder.

He shrugged in response.

"If someone got to Juliette, then they could get to any of us. Hotels like that have great security. It's just too much! Whoever did this could come for any one of us next!"

"Is this real?" whispered Maeve. She was convinced this was a performance for her benefit, fabricated to draw her away from asking any more questions.

"I saw her in a made-for-tv movie a few years back," Jordan responded. "She can't act. If this was fake, we'd know."

"I'm sorry," Alexa said again, wiping her nose on Maeve's blazer. "I just can't believe they're both gone. Life is so short. Too short to be angry at the people you care about."

"I'm so sorry, Ms. Kyle," said Maeve, giving her a soft pat on the back. "We didn't mean to upset you."

"You know, the grief, it makes the singing better. That's what my mother believed."

"Okay," Maeve said, pulling herself away from Alexa's hug. "If you can tell us where you were two nights ago, and then during the time of death of Emily eight days ago, then we can let you get back to your rehearsal."

"I had performances both nights. I went out with my producer two nights ago, eight days ago… that would have been a Wednesday? I was out with the band. We went to a bar not far from here."

"Thank you for your time," Maeve said, as she wrote all that down. They would have to double check this, but between the overblown tears and this response, Maeve's suspicions were decreasing.

"I've seen a lot," Maeve told Jordan, as they walked back to the main hall of the casino, "but I've never been cried on."

"You'll get used to it," he responded.

"Well," Maeve said, "there has to be someone else who connects these two."

Jordan gave a reassuring nod, and the two of them stepped back into his car.

"It's only a matter of time before we find it," he reassured her.

"If we don't, then someone else is bound to get hurt," Maeve said, knowing that in cases like this, time was of the essence. Every minute the killer was on the loose was another minute that the city was in danger.

"Not to mention, Kirk Cavendish will make sure we never work another case again."

CHAPTER SIXTEEN

The woman smiled to herself as she walked down the strip the next morning.

The Las Vegas strip in the daylight is a bustling scene, with towering hotels and casinos lining both sides of the street. The bright sunlight reflects off the glass windows and glistens on the metal structures, creating a shimmering effect. The sidewalks are crowded with people, vendors selling their wares, and street performers entertaining the passersby.

Still, something was different about today.

There was a tension that hung in the air.

She couldn't help but feel a swell of pride, knowing that she was responsible for the shockwave hitting the city. Once again, the passersby were none the wiser to who she was or what she had done.

Just that morning, the media had broken their long silence about Juliette— a silence she suspected was paid for by Kirk Cavendish. The murder of Juliette had rocked people to their core. Celebrities and performers were already posting phony goodbyes to social media.

In the last report she read, the FBI were only beginning to investigate a possible connection to the mysterious but “accidental” death of Emily Smith.

But not one single soul suspected the person who was truly responsible.

She had been too careful for that.

Better than that, no one would find her next victim for days. She’d left the most recent body in yet another hotel room. Afraid that it would allow the FBI to catch up to her, in a stroke of genius, she put a "do not disturb” sign on the door. No one would even dare knock until the guest's checkout was long overdue.

Murder, as it turned out, wasn’t that hard.

All you needed was to put in a little thought, leave no trace behind, and the city would do the rest. No one was looking for her, no one even had a clue who she was.

She was running circles around the FBI.

Everyone always underestimated her. They overlooked her.

They always had.

She was made to be invisible, but that was finally her greatest advantage.

Her phone buzzed in her pocket, interrupting her thoughts. She pulled it out to find a call from her employer. Nick.

In spite of herself, her face went warm at the sight of his name.

"Hello?" she said, adjusting her hair so that it fell over her shoulders in just the right way.

"Hey," he greeted her. His voice sounded short and urgent, his tone was hushed. "Where are you?" he asked.

"Nowhere," she answered. The cryptic message might have sounded a little overly friendly, maybe even flirtatious.

Nick, like always, was oblivious. "Have you heard about what is going on? I just saw it on the news. Juliette and Emily?"

"I know! I'm just so heartbroken," she said, forcing some sadness into her voice. It was hard to do while smiling from ear to ear. "It's such a tragedy."

"They're saying it's murder, did you know that?"

"I heard something like that for Juliette's death. I'm still in shock."

There was a moment of silence, and she heard him breathing on the other side of the line. She wondered where he was. At this hour, he probably wasn't even out of bed yet.

"I need you to be honest with me. Can you do that for me?" he asked.

"Of course, Nick," she said.

"Do you know anything about this, anything at all?"

She knew she couldn't trust him with the truth. Nick wouldn't understand. He was always so oblivious.

What was one more lie?

"Nick, you know me. I don't know anything about this. I'm as much in the dark as you are," she said, her voice cracking a little. She reminded herself that she should feel scared in this situation. That she shouldn't come across confused, sad, frightened.

"Okay," he said, his voice softening. "I'm sorry, I'm just worried about you. Just be careful, okay? This city is crazy. You know how fast this stuff gets around. If someone found out that I–"

He stopped himself, even though they both knew what he was about to say.

"I'll be careful, Nick. Don't worry about me," she said, though the thought of it was a bit sweet. After all this time was he finally starting to care?

But it was too late for that.

"Nick, I'm more worried about you," she continued. "You know how it is, with your job, your... involvement. Maybe you should lay low for a little while."

He sighed. "I know. I just can't shake the feeling that I need to be doing something to help. You know how it is."

"I do," she said, her voice soothing. "But you have to be careful. The cops, they wouldn't understand. I've been keeping tabs on them. One of them is Maeve Sharp, and she's here all the way from FBI headquarters on the east coast. They're not messing around, I think Juliette's dad got involved. I don't want anything to happen to you."

There was a pause. She could hear the sound of traffic in the background. Maybe he was walking to the nearest café for breakfast. "I know," he said finally. "I'll be careful. You take care of yourself, okay?"

"I will," she said. "But I don't have anything to worry about. I wasn't close with them."

"And one last thing... the FBI... they've already talked to Alexa Kyle."

"Oh, have they?" She was a little surprised, a little bit impressed.

Maeve Sharp and her new partner were moving a little faster than she expected. She would have to keep it up with her regular precautions.

"You don't think it could be her, do you?"

"I wouldn't know, Nick," she said, with another smile creeping across her lips. "I just can't understand why anyone would do this to someone else. Emily and Juliette of all people."

"You truly are one of the kindest people I know," Nick said. "That's why I know I can trust you. We should talk soon. In person."

"Of course," she said, and he hung up the phone.

She almost jumped for joy in the middle of the street. Everything was going exactly as she planned.

CHAPTER SEVENTEEN

Maeve and Jordan sat hunched over in the dimly lit briefing room, their faces illuminated only by the glow of the laptops and phones strewn across the table.

The atmosphere was tense, with a sense of urgency permeating the room as they delved deep into the case files. The sound of rustling paper filled the air as they sifted through countless documents and photos, desperate for any clue that could lead them to a breakthrough. They had been working on this case for what felt like an eternity, and the lack of progress was starting to wear on them. Maeve knew that the other cases hadn't been easy, but something about working a case here was particularly draining.

She rubbed her temples, feeling the beginnings of a headache forming as she tried to piece together the scattered fragments of information. Jordan let out a frustrated sigh, running a hand through his hair as he scanned through another report.

They had already called on every resource they had, from their fellow agents to forensic specialists, but still they were coming up empty-handed. The clock was ticking, and the pressure was mounting. Would they ever find the missing piece of the puzzle that would finally crack the case wide open?

Maeve leaned back in her chair and let out a sigh. "This is getting us nowhere." She tugged at a strand of her hair.

Jordan took off his glasses and began cleaning them on his shirt sleeve. He stared at the whiteboard with a dazed look in his eye, and then turned to where all the information and pictures associated with the case had been pinned. "We need to find a connection, some kind of lead. But what?"

"I just don't understand it," Maeve said, frustration clear in her voice. "We've considered every possibility. Every eventuality. And we're still stuck."

"He knows what he's doing, targeting these women. The killer knows that very little can be traced back to him," Jordan said. He hadn't given up on the assumption that the killer was a man, and had already explained to Maeve how statistically speaking, it was almost unfathomable that the victims were killed by a woman.

Maeve was just about to tell him that even the toughest cases she worked in Virginia didn't stall like this, when her phone rang.

A number she didn't recognize lit up the screen.

"I have to take this," she said, pushing herself out of her swivel chair and leaving the room.

She rushed to the stairwell on the other side of the floor, where no one would be able to hear her. Who could be calling? Surely it wasn't something to do with the case?

Safely in the stairwell, she opened her phone and picked up the call. "Hello?" she said, trying to make her voice sound clear, and not as tired as she felt.

"Ms. Sharp?" said a woman's voice on the other end.

"Yes?"

"I have some bad news. It's about your mother."

Maeve's heart rate spiked. She felt like her stomach had been loaded with bricks.

"What's going on?" she said. "Is everything okay?"

"There's no need to panic..." said the woman on the other end. "I'm one of the hospice nurses assigned to your mother's case. She is stabilizing now so there's no need to be worried."

No need to be worried? This nurse clearly didn't have the best bedside manner.

Maeve's senses went dull as the nurse spoke. She tried to wrap her head around what was being said.

"But there was an incident earlier today. She was found on the floor of her room, unresponsive. We're not sure how long she had been there before we found her."

The nurse explained more, but her medical jargon, with words like "comatose" and "seizure," hardly landed on Maeve. Instead her mind went blank.

The only thing she could think about was her mother's body, limp on the floor. She knew her mother's condition was fragile, but she never expected this.

"What happened? Is she going to be okay?" Maeve interrupted the nurse, mid-explanation.

"As you know," said the nurse, "your mother's condition is very serious. The tumor is putting a lot of pressure on her brainstem. She's already so weak; she's lucky a stroke like this didn't kill her."

"I'm on my way now," Maeve said. This nurse wasn't telling her what she needed to hear.

Maeve was already digging in her pockets for her car keys. If she took backroads, then she could be there in under an hour…

"She's resting now. She won't be awake for several more hours. She needs as much sleep as possible. If you come home now, you won't be able to talk to her. And like I said, she's stable. I heard you're an investigator? For the FBI?"

The nurse paused and waited for Maeve to respond.

When she didn't, she continued with, "That sounds really important, so you should focus on that as much as you can. You don't need to worry about anything for the time being. I just wanted to let you know."

Maeve let out a long breath. She wanted to go home, but knew she wouldn't be any use to her mother from there. "Thank you for letting me know," she said, her voice unsteady. "Please keep me updated."

"Of course," said the nurse, before hanging up.

Maeve slumped back against the wall, listening to the sound of her voice echo through the stairwell. This case was already taking a toll on her, and now with her mother's health rapidly declining...

She wasn't sure how much more she could handle.

She felt a lump in her throat that she couldn't swallow down. Her relationship with her dad was so fraught that the idea of losing her mom felt like losing everything.

No matter what she told herself, no matter how she tried to prepare, she still wasn't ready.

She wanted to get in the car and go home, regardless of the nurse's advice. Even if her mother was still asleep when she got there, she could be there for her when she woke up. She could be there to answer her questions, to comfort her.

Maybe she would even bake cookies, like they used to together on Saturday afternoons, to cheer her up.

Maeve's mother had been there for her through every major event in her life. Every time she fell, her mom was there to pull her back up again.

Maeve hated that, now that her mother needed her the most, she was too busy with a pressing case to be there for her in return.

But deep down she knew the nurse was right…

She had a sneaking suspicion that she was more valuable to the world as a detective. And her mother's baking skills were never really passed on.

She would give her mom space now, space to rest as much as she needed. And when the case was finally over… if it ever ended… she would focus her full attention on her mom then. For the time being, there was nothing more she could do.

Maeve took a deep breath and tried to ground herself in the present moment, the case, and its frustrating lack of leads.

She had to do what she did best— channel her pain into her work.

The only person she could help was the killer's next target.

Maeve was still misty-eyed when she entered the briefing room and sank back into her chair. Jordan sat in the same place, crouched over his laptop, looking at a file Maeve hadn't seen before. She took a deep breath before speaking.

"Sorry for the interruption," she said. "What have we got so far?"

Jordan looked up at her, eyebrows raised. "Is everything okay?"

Maeve wondered if he would understand, but decided against burdening him with her personal problems. Even if she were to tell him, where would she begin?

"Yeah," she said. "I just had to take a quick call."

He looked like he didn't believe her, but he turned back to the whiteboard anyway.

"We've gone over everything again and again, but we can't seem to find a connection between Emily, Juliette, and any potential suspects."

Maeve furrowed her brow. "What about their personal lives? Relationships, enemies, anything?"

"We've looked into everything," Jordan looked at the floor and shook his head. "No one seems to have had any reason to harm them."

Maeve rubbed her forehead, feeling a headache coming on.

"There has to be something we're missing," she said. "How much longer do we have until we can get the phones unlocked?"

"A few more days."

"We can't wait that long."

The two sat in silence for a moment, until Jordan swiveled in his chair, fingers flying over his laptop, as he pulled up employee records from both hotels.

"What is it?" Maeve asked.

"Just a second…" he said, not looking up from his screen. "I've got to be sure."

Maeve leaned over his shoulder, trying to see what he was looking at, but the personnel records didn't mean anything to her without the context of what Jordan was looking for.

"Just tell me," she pushed.

"You're going to love this," he looked up at her with a smirk on his face. "We've been thinking about this whole case from the outside looking in, but what if we just need to take a step back? Stop thinking about the people and who they knew, why someone would want to kill them. What if we needed to think more practically?”

“Like who had access to both hotel rooms,” Maeve said, slightly angry that she didn’t think of this sooner.

“I cross-referenced all the staff of both hotels and found something. Selina Hargrove worked at both hotels. She's a casino manager. I know it isn't much, but maybe she had some knowledge of their security? She could have been able to get in and out of both rooms without being detected. She still works at the second casino."

Maeve squinted at the small ID photo on Jordan’s screen. She pursed her lips, eager for the case to pick up, but not wanting to get her hopes up too soon.

"That's a great find, Jordan. Let's go talk to her."

The two detectives raced to the car, and Jordan drove them away from the field office, towards the strip.

As they passed the familiar buildings of the city, fast approaching another potential murderer, Maeve couldn’t help but think of her mother, lying motionless on her bed, getting weaker by the hour.

It wasn’t just the killer’s next strike that she was racing against. Until she finished this case, she would never have enough time to go home and see her mother. And she realized she had a lot less time than she thought.

CHAPTER EIGHTEEN

As Maeve and Jordan approached the casino, the neon lights and buzzing energy of Las Vegas overwhelmed them. The slot machines created a symphony of sound, punctuated by the occasional shriek of a winner. It was hard to believe that just a few days ago, they had walked through the same casino in silence, searching for clues.

Maeve couldn't help but feel a sense of frustration as they walked past the glittering slot machines. It was as if the casino-goers were oblivious to the tragedy that had occurred just a few feet away.

"I can't believe these people tried to cover up a murder, and they just got away with it," Maeve said. "Now it is just business as usual."

Maeve turned to the first person she could find-- a security guard standing at the door.

The security guard appeared to be in his early forties. He was tall, balding, and had a broad chest. His eyes were a dull blue and his face, like all those around him, was void of emotion, making it hard to read him.

The security guard was a big man, at least six-foot-three. He had a thick neck and broad shoulders, muscles so thick they strained against his shirt. His face was wide, with dark brown eyes and thinning dark hair.

The man was dressed in a blue uniform with gold buttons and had a large belt buckle with a snake on it.

"FBI," she said, maybe a little too loudly, too spitefully, her voice carrying a tone of determination as she announced their presence and purpose. “We’re here to investigate someone in connection to the murder of Emily Smith and Juliette Cavendish."

As they entered Selina's office, Maeve was struck by the stark contrast between the noisy, bustling casino floor and the quiet, sterile environment of the office. The walls were painted a light shade of blue, with framed certificates and diplomas hung neatly in a row behind Selina's desk. The room was cool and dimly lit, with a subtle hum of the air conditioning system in the background.

The scent of lavender and peppermint filled the air, likely from the essential oil diffuser sitting on a shelf next to a vase of fresh flowers.

Maeve took a deep breath, feeling the calming effect of the scents and the quietness of the room.

But the emptiness of the room was jarring. Selina's desk was tidy, with a computer monitor, a notepad, and a pen placed precisely in the center. The drawers were closed, and the cabinets were organized with labeled folders. It was almost as if Selina had never been there at all.

Jordan strode over to the computer, turning it on and trying to access any information that could lead them to Selina. Maeve looked around the room, inspecting every nook and cranny, hoping to find some clue that would bring them closer to solving the case.

She noticed a framed photo on Selina's desk, showing her with two other women, all dressed in formal attire and holding glasses of champagne. Maeve picked up the photo and examined it more closely, studying the faces of the women. But try as she might, she couldn't shake off the feeling of unease in the empty office. Something was definitely off, and Maeve couldn't help but wonder where Selina was and what she was up to.

"What exactly is Selina's role here?" Maeve asked the security guard, who watched them vigilantly as the two detectives circled the office.

"Casino manager," he explained.

"And is she well liked?" Maeve asked.

"Selina is good at her job," he answered. "And that's all that's really needed of her. I have noticed that she's not the kindest to the other people around her."

"In what way?" Jordan pushed.

The guard frowned. "I really don't want to get involved," he said. "I thought it was wrong, how they handled what happened to Emily. But I don't want to talk bad about my coworkers."

"Anything you tell us will be strictly confidential," Maeve assured him. "We just want to find out who is responsible. That's it."

"Well, I often noticed that Selina wasn't nicer to the younger women who worked here. I don't know why. She's always treated me really well, but she talked to Emily like she was dirt. She used to call her names, and make her run meaningless errands. Like she was trying to make her feel less than. It always bothered me, but I never thought it could be related to something darker."

Maeve took this in slowly. By the neat arrangement of her office and the stories from this guard, she seemed shiftier by the moment.

"And where is Selina now?" asked Maeve.

"I have no idea."

"She didn't take time off?"

"No. She never showed up to work today at all."

Maeve looked at Jordan. This was just the kind of behavior they looked for in suspects for a case.

"Is that unusual?"

"Well," he said hesitantly. "I wouldn't say it's out of the question. She has a tendency to storm off when she gets angry. But not coming in at all... that is new."

Maeve frowned. "We're going to need her home address."

***

As the two drove towards Selina's house, Maeve kept thinking of her mother. She tried to push the thoughts away. Maeve knew she couldn't let her personal life distract her from the case, but her mother's health was weighing heavily on her mind. She made a mental note to check in with the hospice nurse every chance she got.

"Look, I know you said that everything's alright..." began Jordan. "But I just want you to know that if you ever need to talk…"

"Thanks," said Maeve. "Just some family issues."

She appreciated the thought, but she hoped he would drop it.

"I know how it is," said Jordan.

Maeve looked at him closely when he said this, wondering if he meant it.

The two drove through the Las Vegas suburbs towards Selina Hargrove's house. The streets were quiet, a stark contrast to the bright lights and noise of the strip. They pulled up to a sprawling house with a well-manicured lawn and a fancy car parked in the driveway.

As they approached the front door, Maeve's stomach tightened with nerves. This was the moment they had been working towards for weeks, and she couldn't help but feel a sense of apprehension.

After a moment, Selina answered the door, her expression cool and unwelcoming. She was a middle-aged woman with striking features. Her sharp jawline and high cheekbones gave her an air of authority, and her piercing blue eyes seemed to see right through Maeve and Jordan. She was dressed in a sharp suit that fit her toned body perfectly, and her blonde hair was styled into a sleek bob. Despite her impressive appearance, there was a coldness to her demeanor that sent a chill down Maeve's spine.

Maeve introduced themselves as FBI agents investigating the murders of Emily Smith and Juliette Cavendish, and asked if they could ask her a few questions.

Selina's eyes narrowed and her tone turned chilly. "I've already spoken to the police," she said. "I don't see why I need to talk to you."

"You had access to both of their hotel rooms," said Jordan.

"I work at a casino. A lot of people had access to those rooms. What are you implying?"

"Selina," Maeve said, her voice gentle but firm. "We understand that this is a difficult situation for you, but we need to ask these questions to get a better understanding of what happened. Can you tell us more about your relationship with Emily and Juliette?"

Selina sighed, her guard dropping slightly. "We worked together for several years, so we were friendly. But like I said, we weren't close."

Maeve nodded. “And what can you tell us about the people Emily hung out with? Did she have many friends? Can you think of anyone who would want to hurt her?"

Selina pressed her thin lips together. “Why don’t you try asking that boyfriend of hers. He was always distracting her from her work.”

There was a clear tone of jealousy as she spoke, in the way that she pursed her lips and spat the words.

“According to Alexa Kyle, Emily was very dedicated. And she didn’t mention anything about a boyfriend.”

“That’s because it was a secret,” Selina said. “But Emily wasn’t smart enough to keep a secret like that very well.”

“Could you give us a name?” Maeve said. She suspected that this was just a bluff, a red herring to throw her off and waste her time.

“Of course not,” she snapped. “I’m perceptive, but I’m not a diviner.”

Jordan leaned forward onto the doorframe. He looked as unconvinced as Maeve felt. "Did they ever seem scared or worried about anything?"

Selina paused for a moment, her brow furrowing. "Now that you mention it, Emily did seem a bit stressed out lately. But she never told me what was going on."

Maeve and Jordan exchanged a look. This was a significant development. If Emily was feeling stressed, it could mean that she was in danger or that something was going on that she wasn't comfortable sharing.

“What about Juliette Cavendish? You worked at her hotel as well.”

"I didn't keep any of the keycards to the rooms, if that's what you're asking."

"I wasn't asking that," Maeve said, noting how defensive this woman was.

Jordan's phone rang before Maeve could ask another question, and he stepped away into Selina's front yard to answer it.

"Why did you miss work today?" Maeve asked. She tried to look past Selina into her house, to see if it looked like she was packing up her belongings, getting ready to run.

"A little under the weather."

Maeve frowned. "Can I get your contact information, in case we have more questions?" Maeve asked.

Jordan nodded her over from the lawn. "Sharp, we've got to go," he said.

Maeve waited for Selina to finish writing out her phone number before following him back into the car.

"She's certainly suspicious," said Maeve, getting back into the car. "Why did you do that? I was just about to get more information."

"Because that was Williams," Jordan said, starting the ignition. "They've found another body."

Maeve felt suddenly chilled to the bone.

"If it is the same killer… and the signs indicate that it is… then we have a serial killer on our hands."

Maeve leaned back against the seat behind her, and watched the suburbs fade away. They were headed back to the heart of the city, where the new victim was left.

She knew that she hadn't been fast enough. She needed to work harder. To put this killer away before someone else got hurt.

"We'll catch them," Jordan said, as if reading her thoughts. "We just need to keep working at it."

Maeve nodded, but deep down, she knew that this case was unlike any she had worked on before, and the killer seemed to be one step ahead of them at every turn. But she couldn't let that stop her. Lives were at stake, and she was determined to catch the perpetrator before they struck again.

CHAPTER NINETEEN

The two arrived at the new crime scene after dark. The seedy motel was a far cry from the upscale hotels of the city, with only blinking fluorescent street lamps to illuminate it to the people driving by. There was a half-filled pool around the back that had long since turned green with algae. The brick facade was cracking halfway up the building, and Maeve could smell an unpleasant concoction of weed, alcohol, and gasoline as she stepped out of the car. The parking lot was already full of police cruisers and a forensics team, winding crime scene tape across a door on the lower level. Their red and blue lights lit up the sky, forcing Maeve to squint.

Maeve ducked under the crime scene tape and stepped inside the room, already crowded with police milling around, taking photos, and collecting evidence.

An ashtray in the middle of the room was still smoking with the latter half of a cigarette, and the carpeted floor was stained with various shades of brown and red. The walls were a dingy shade of yellow and peeling wallpaper revealed glimpses of old floral patterns.

The furniture was old and worn, with tears and cigarette burns on the upholstery. A small television sat on a rickety wooden stand, playing a late-night infomercial before Maeve had a chance to put on a latex glove so she could pick up the remote and shut it off. The room's only source of light came from a flickering lamp in the corner, casting long shadows across the room.

The bed was unmade, with rumpled sheets and a stained comforter. A discarded cocktail dress lay on the floor, along with a crumpled pack of cigarettes and an empty condom wrapper. The room had a feeling of emptiness to it, as if it had seen its fair share of heartbreak and desperation. It was the kind of place where people went to forget their problems, but found only more trouble.

Jordan followed in after Maeve, taking a long look at the cluttered room around them. He approached the detective in charge of the crime scene, a gruff-looking man with a bushy mustache holding a cup of coffee.

"Agent Jordan, FBI," he said. “What do we have?"

Maeve pushed her way past another officer so she could hear the update too.

"Daniels," the detective introduced himself, taking a hesitant sip of his coffee. He shook his head, and stared with a blank expression into the middle distance. "Homicide. Pretty clear."

"Tell us about the victim," Maeve said.

"Her name is Adrienne Howe, 22 years old. Out-of-towner."

Maeve felt a sinking feeling in her stomach. It was already unlikely that this new victim had any connection to Selina.

But Selina was her best suspect.

She didn't know how to make this new information fit into the rest of the case.

"This matches the MO of a killer we've been investigating. We're going to need to take over the case," Maeve said.

"Be my guest," he said, with an apathetic shrug.

"Okay, I need everyone to clear the room," announced Jordan. "Everyone except forensics."

A few of the officers grumbled as they slowly filed away. A few of them looked upset to lose an important case, but most of them just seemed relieved to be allowed to go home to their families. Daniels lingered behind, with his coffee cup in hand. Maeve could see the details of the scene better now that there was more room to move around.

Unlike the other crime scenes, the body in this one had not been moved yet.

Maeve had avoided looking directly at her, but she knew she couldn't avoid it any longer.

Looking at photos of a body in a crime scene was one thing, but being in the same room… that was another thing entirely.

Maeve forced herself to lean in, not to step away.

She walked closer to the bed and examined the victim's body.

The young woman was lying on her back, arms spread wide, as if she had been crucified. Her eyes were open, staring blankly at the ceiling, and her mouth was slightly agape as if caught in a silent scream. There were bruises around her neck where the killer had strangled her to death.

The young woman had a heart-shaped face with delicate features, her soft brown hair falling in loose waves around her shoulders. She had a petite frame, with a slender waist and graceful limbs.

Maeve's eyes lingered on the woman's face, and she felt a surge of anger and sadness wash over her. This was someone's daughter, someone's sister, someone's friend. Even the FBI knew little about her and what had brought her here, to such a broken place. And now she was just another victim of a senseless crime.

She felt a sudden pang of grief.

And then a stronger wave of guilt washed over her.

Maeve was responsible for protecting women like Adrienne. She knew that there was a killer on the loose, and she hadn't been able to stop them before Adrienne was added to the list of victims. The people of Las Vegas trusted law enforcement to protect the streets.

Only time would tell if this was indeed the same killer, as expected; but with strangulation as a rare cause of death in this city, the coincidence was hard to ignore.

A forensic investigator spread a white, sheet-like tarp over her before Maeve could look any longer.

Maeve pulled aside one of the few officers who had been allowed to stay inside the room. "We need to start canvassing the area," she said. "Talk to anyone who might have seen something suspicious."

The detective nodded, "Already on it. But so far, nothing."

"What about security footage?" Maeve asked.

"It's a cheap motel," he said with a shrug. "People don't exactly come here if they think they might be recorded. I'll look into it, but I'd be shocked if they have a camera on anything other than the register."

Maeve surveyed the scene, trying to see if there was anything that stood out to her. But everything looked the same as the other crime scenes—a young woman's lifeless body, posed on the bed.

The murder weapon was still wound around her neck— a nylon cord just like in the other murders. It had a heavy buckle on one end.

The other murders had been gruesome, but this one felt like a slap in the face.

Jordan nodded, his expression grim. "Let's keep working the case and see if we can find any leads."

"How do you know it's your guy?" said Daniels, returning from outside, coffee cup still in hand.

"Tell us more about the victim," said Maeve, "and then we'll know for sure."

But the detective sipped his coffee as he said, "Nothing so far. We're still getting credit cards and phone records, but both could take a while. She paid for the room in cash."

"Cash?" said Jordan. "That's unusual."

"It's a cash city," said Daniels. "Doesn't always mean that you're hiding something."

"What about the locks on the doors?"

"There was no forced entry," Daniels added.

"Money clearly isn't a motive in this case," Maeve said. "Anything could have been taken from Juliette's penthouse, but wasn't. If you ignore the level of the hotel, all the other details remain the same. It's the same killer. It has to be. The victims are all too similar, the cause of death, too."

Jordan nodded in agreement.

"Do you think they knew him?" Daniels asked.

"We're not sure it is a him," Maeve said, thinking of Selina, who was still her best suspect.

"It's hard to say," Jordan answered Daniels. "In the higher-end hotel rooms, the killer could have used the guise of room service or housekeeping to get into the room. A stolen card key would have done the trick too. But this... I don't know. I suppose someone could have pretended to bring a delivery?"

Maeve nodded. The women were most likely murdered by someone that they trusted. Someone that they opened their hotel doors to without question.

Maeve examined belongings found with the body—all simple and minimalistic. Even the choice of the motel room itself was a stark contrast from the other crime scenes.

"What connects these women?" she wondered. "Think about it—Juliette was one of the most high-profile women in the whole city, killed in her penthouse apartment. It was practically her home. Emily was staying in a nice place too, but this... It doesn't make sense."

"What about the mystery boyfriend that Selina talked about?" Jordan said. "Do you think he could be involved?"

"I certainly can't rule it out," Maeve said, angry at such a vague lead. "But she could have been lying. Once we examine the room, then we'll know more."

Maeve examined everything around her closely. She found that Adrienne had left behind a half-empty suitcase made of suede, filled with dresses and a few hundred dollar bills.

"Looks like someone was planning to gamble," said Daniels, as Maeve placed it all in a new evidence bag.

"I'm going to keep looking around," she said.

Her bathroom was full of drugstore lipstick and dirty clothes. She also found a few pieces of jewelry on the counter but these didn't match the surroundings. There was a gold locket that must have been at least ten karats, a family heirloom of some kind by the looks of it.

As Maeve examined the bathroom, something caught her eye. Next to a dozen other posters and flyers, a flier for a magic show was taped to the mirror. The name of the magician sounded familiar— The Artful Dodger. A cheesy stage name no doubt, but there was something about his face, his dark hair and olive skin, which looked familiar.

But it certainly wasn't a lead.

Without wasting any time, Maeve snapped a photo of the flier with her phone and made a note to follow up on it later. She took more pictures of the scene, making note of all the flyers, takeout menus, and other items found in the room. If leads went cold again, maybe she could reach out to some of the people displayed on the papers.

As she turned to leave the room, she was forced to look at the whole crime scene again, along with the vague imprint of the body on the other side of the tarp. She quickly pushed the feeling aside, telling herself that she was just tired and overworked.

Her fists tightened.

She felt tears threatening to roll down her cheeks.

With every passing moment, Maeve was failing Juliette and Emily, and now, Adrienne too.

If she had been a better detective, maybe she would have caught the culprit by now.

Maybe Adrienne would still be alive.

"Hey," said Jordan, following her out of the hotel. He placed a calming hand on her shoulder.

"I've been thinking. You should go home. Get some rest. Come back in the morning with a clear head. We've been working this case nonstop."

"No," Maeve refused.

Why was he saying this to her? Did he think that she didn't have what it took to finish the job?

"I know what I'm doing," she said.

But if she was honest with herself, she was beginning to lose faith.

What if this was the case that beat her?

Her father used to tell her that every detective had one—a case they couldn’t solve, couldn’t recover from.

This was exactly what happened with Veronica. Maeve had read her case, searched her sister's life a hundred times, but found no trace after her disappearance.

What if she wasn't smart enough, skilled enough? Not just for Adrienne, but for her own sister too.

Real people were counting on her to do her job.

"I know," Jordan said. "I have faith in you. I just want you to think about getting some rest. That's all."

Maeve shook her head again. "I have to finish this. I don't care if I die trying."

CHAPTER TWENTY

On the drive back from the hotel, Jordan drove through the strip once again. Now the lights only seemed to be taunting Maeve, as she watched absently as people flooded the streets.

"All I'm saying is that it's okay," said Jordan from the driver's seat. She hadn't been paying attention to him for the drive. She couldn't focus on anything, other than the image of Adrienne on that motel room bed.

"What?" she asked, as his voice came back into focus.

"If the case goes cold," he repeated. "It happens... sometimes."

She waited for him to add a snarky but not to me, but the comment never came.

Maybe, after all the pridefulness of the last two days, he had finally begun to care. If he was being genuine now, then he must have been really worried. Maeve was starting to trust him.

He had been a good partner, all things considered.

But she couldn't stand the idea of the case going cold.

The idea made her clench her fists and her face turn hot with anger.

"Sometimes there's nothing that the detectives can do. I mean, we never even got to see the second crime scene. And that's not our fault. Maeve, are you listening?"

But she had tuned him out again, and instead she was only thinking about how she was going to make a breakthrough in the case.

"I just want you to know that it's okay. It's not your fault."

"Oh, it's okay? It's okay that these people's families never get justice? That their families never get closure? It's okay to just leave our jobs half finished?"

She slumped deeper into the passenger's seat and folded her arms.

She saw Jordan looking at her suspiciously out of the corner of her eye.

"I didn't mean that," she said. "I didn't mean to snap. I'm just tired."

"I didn't mean it either," he said. "I just wanted you to get some rest. That's all."

"I don't need rest," she said. "I need to solve the case. Pull over."

"What? Why? Do you need to stop and get something?"

He turned again, his eyebrows raising in concern above the frames of his glasses.

"Just pull over," she said, with a stern voice. "I just need to think. If I can clear my head, maybe I can think my way out of this."

He gave an exasperated sigh. "Are you sure... you probably shouldn't be alone here..."

"I grew up here," Maeve reminded him. "I'll be fine."

With no other choice, Jordan brought the car to the curb, and Maeve stepped out onto the sidewalk.

Without looking back at him, she walked away.

The lights were a blur of vibrant colors, flickering incessantly, drawing her attention away from her thoughts. It was as if the city had a life of its own, a pulse that beat rhythmically with the thump of her heart. The people around her were in a rush, bustling to get to their destinations, oblivious to her internal turmoil.

Maeve walked past a street magician, his audience mesmerized by his sleight of hand. She couldn't bring herself to stop and watch, though. She was too consumed by the case, too consumed by the fact that a killer was on the loose and that she had yet to make any headway.

As she walked, Maeve noticed a dark alleyway, tucked between two towering buildings. A flicker of movement caught her eye, and she paused, straining to see what it was.

But it was too dark, too deep, too dangerous.

A shiver ran down her spine as she imagined what could be lurking in the shadows. The thought of the killer being so close sent her heart racing. She had to find a way to stop them, to end the reign of terror that had been unleashed on the city.

As she walked, Maeve couldn't help but feel defeated. She had been working tirelessly, and yet the killer still seemed to elude her. Every lead she followed turned into a dead end; every witness she interviewed gave her nothing but vague and unhelpful information.

Even Selina's suspicious behavior didn't fit what she expected of the killer.

The constant chaos of the strip only added to her frustration. The bright lights, the flashing billboards, and the endless crowds were overwhelming. Maeve couldn't shake the feeling that she was just a small fish in a big pond, hopelessly out of her depth.

But as she walked, she reminded herself why she was here. She wasn't just a detective; she was a protector. Her job was to keep the people of this city safe, to stop this killer from hurting anyone else.

The night air was cool, and Maeve's breath came out in small puffs as she walked. She kept her eyes peeled, alert for any sign of danger. Her hand instinctively went to her gun, a comforting weight against her hip.

Despite her weariness, Maeve knew she couldn't give up. The killer was out there somewhere, and she was the only one who could stop them. With a deep breath, she continued down the strip, determined to see this case through to the end.

She was so lost in thought that the city seemed to vanish, along with the crowds of people. The sound faded away, and it was like Maeve walked all alone down those familiar, dirty sidewalks.

Then she suddenly walked straight into a street performer, making him drop two of his flaming batons.

"I'm so sorry," she said instinctually, snapped back to the present moment.

She looked up at the man whose show she had just interrupted. He was tall, and shirtless, showing off a gallery of colorful tattoos all over his chest. He wore an old top hat that looked like it had been purchased from a cheap costume store. He was coated in the smell of fire, wood burning, mingled with sweat.

She tried to maneuver her way around the crowd that encircled him, but she was trapped.

He retrieved his batons almost as quickly as he had dropped them. "Watch where you're going, lady!" he yelled, his voice thick with annoyance.

Maeve stumbled back, apologizing profusely, but the performer wasn't having any of it. He continued to berate her, the heat from the flames making her feel even more uncomfortable.

"Little lady wants to join the performance," he yelled to his crowd. "Do they teach juggling in... finance school?" he guessed, from the uptight nature of her outfit.

"I said I'm sorry," Maeve said.

Finally, he turned back to his performance, and Maeve quickly made her way out of the crowd, her face burning with embarrassment.

She walked away, still feeling the performer's angry gaze on her back. As she continued down the strip, she couldn't shake the feeling of frustration that had been gnawing at her all night. She was supposed to be making progress in the case, but it seemed like every lead was a dead end. And now, to top it all off, she had made a fool of herself in front of a group of strangers.

As she walked, the lights and sounds of the strip blurred together, creating a surreal atmosphere. She felt a sense of disorientation, as if she were lost in a dream.

She remembered a distant day when she and Veronica had skipped school together and come to the strip.

They had walked hand-in-hand, marveling at the bright lights and glitz that surrounded them. They had been carefree then, with no worries weighing down their hearts.

Maeve could still see her sister's face, brimming with joy when Maeve agreed to drive the two of them to one of the casinos instead of to school.

Perhaps it wasn't the best example that Maeve had ever set for her sister, but they both had been having a hard time making friends, and she wanted to forget her troubles by losing all her quarters to the slot machines.

By sheer luck, the two won back more money and used it to go to lunch at one of the upscale restaurants in the hotel. All the older adults around them clearly knew they were skipping school, but no one seemed to care.

They never even told their parents, arriving home at the exact same time as the school bus.

At the time, Maeve thought that she would regret missing class and teaching her sister to avoid her problems. But now, memories like these were the most precious to her. The whole day was a secret that she still kept, all these years later.

Even with its darkness, its licentiousness, this was a place of happiness and joy.

As long as you didn't let the luster of the casinos pull you in too deep, the flashing lights and bubbling fountains were an enjoyable experience for anyone.

But the thought of it caused Maeve to pause in her steps.

Had the three victims been able to feel joy before their untimely end?

She remembered a picture of Juliette, one of the few in which she looked truly happy, just before she had died. It was uploaded on a tabloid blog, and showed her, beaming ear-to-ear, as she left the show of an escape artist.

But there was a deeper layer to the photo. Maeve stopped in the middle of the sidewalk to pull up the picture online.

She found that it was published with an article, not just on Juliette, but the handsome stranger she had been seen with exiting the show. He had done his best to hide his face, but could it be the performer himself, the skilled escape artist?

The comments on the post were a mile long, all with speculations about Juliette's love life, her relationship to the performers, and other statements to just leave the poor girl alone.

Though the performer's name wasn't given, there was something familiar about his half-hidden smile.

Then Maeve remembered…

The Artful Dodger.

The man in the flier in the third victim's hotel room.

Maeve's heart raced as she realized that all the pieces of the puzzle were finally coming together. The Artful Dodger was a popular escape artist who had performed in Vegas just a few nights before the first murder had occurred.

Could it be possible that the killer was targeting people who had attended his shows?

What if he was the mystery boyfriend?

It was a stretch at best, but she had to follow the lead.

Maeve's mind raced as she considered the possibility. She knew that she had to get to the bottom of this, and fast. She pulled out her phone and called her partner, hoping that he would be able to help her put together the missing pieces.

CHAPTER TWENTY ONE

"Maeve? Where are you... I've been so worried." Jordan's voice on the other end of the phone was distant, blurred with the sound of the streets.

"Can you meet me at the field office?" Maeve said, almost out of breath. "I think I know who did it."

Jordan's tone changed from concern to urgency. "Who? Maeve, tell me."

"Just meet me there as soon as you can."

Maeve hung up before Jordan could argue, and continued down the strip with renewed purpose. She knew that they were closing in on the killer, and she had to move quickly before he struck again.

The Artful Dodger was the only person who made sense. As an escape artist, it would have been easy for him to sneak in and out of hotel rooms, and so far, he was the only person with any kind of connection to all three victims. He had done shows at Emily's hotel, been seen leaving a show with Juliette, and had appeared on a poster in Adrienne's room.

Maeve shook her head. She couldn't jump to conclusions. Not yet.

The connection, though undeniable, was still blurry.

Even though he was connected with all three women, why kill them?

The whole case felt muddled.

She had to stay focused, stay calm, find the solution that fit all the facts.

When she arrived at the field office, Jordan was already there, waiting for her. He looked tired and worn out, but his eyes lit up when he saw her.

"Maeve, you scared me. What's going on?"

Maeve rushed past him towards the briefing room.

"Slow down," he said, walking at top speed to keep up with her. "Are you going to tell me what's going on?"

Maeve switched the lights on, since everyone else had gone home, and pulled a printed photo off the wall.

"Look," she said, pointing at the same picture she had been looking at not an hour before.

"I don't understand," he responded. "It's just another paparazzi photo. Juliette was in a million of them."

"Is that all you see?"

He looked at her blankly. "Yeah?"

"It's not about Juliette," Maeve said, shaking her head. "Look beyond that."

Jordan returned to the picture, scanning it for more details.

"What else do you see in the picture?"

"A sparkly dress?"

Maeve sighed. "The *man* she's with," Maeve pressed. "That half-hidden smile. It's him, Jordan. The Artful Dodger."

"Why does that name sound familiar?" Jordan mused, leaning on the wall next to them. "Oh, yeah. I've read *Oliver Twist* too!"

"Be serious," Maeve told him. "Didn't you see the flier in Adrienne's hotel room?"

Jordan frowned as he studied the photo. "Yeah, but it could be anyone in that photo," he said finally. "We need more than a blurry picture that kind of looks like a guy in a poster to make an arrest."

"I know," Maeve said, frustration creeping into her voice. "But it's a start. And it's more than we had before."

Jordan nodded slowly. "Okay. Let's say, for argument's sake, that it is him. What is the theory? What is the motive?"

Maeve shook her head, piecing together her thoughts.

She had so little to go on. Thinking as hard as she could, she thought of the only explanation that fit the facts.

"All three women were hiding something. What if it was him? What if it was the Artful Dodger?"

"Still think it's a lazy stage name," muttered Jordan.

"What if he was involved with all three of them? The secret boyfriend?"

"You mean he cheated with all of them, and then killed them to cover it up."

"It wouldn't have had to be cheating," Maeve said. "It could be just plain jealousy over an ex. I don't know. He could have had flings with all of them."

"Then why wasn't he spotted the night of the murder?"

"He's an escape artist, for crying out loud. He knows everything about being unnoticed, opening locked doors, wiggling out of tight spaces. Of course he'd be capable of something like this. I'd bet he even uses nylon cord of some sort in his act, maybe as part of the restraints that he has to escape."

Jordan looked thoughtfully into the distance, before finally nodding. "Okay, what's the next step?"

"We need to find out where the Artful Dodger is now," Maeve said. "And we need to find hard evidence if any of this is going to hold up in court. I want to see if we can find any evidence linking him to the crime scenes. We don't even have a name."

Jordan leaned back in his chair, steepling his fingers in front of him as he thought.

They had no name, no face, no leads to go on.

But Maeve had been in the game long enough to know that every criminal leaves a trail, no matter how faint. It was just a matter of following it.

"I'll also reach out to some of our contacts in the city," he continued. "See if anyone has heard of someone matching our suspect's description. Maybe we can get lucky and find someone who's seen him around."

Maeve nodded, her eyes focused on the task at hand. She knew they couldn't waste any time. Lives were on the line, and they were the only ones who could stop this killer.

"I'll go over the reports again," she said. "Maybe there's something we missed, some detail that could lead us to him."

As Maeve scanned more crime scene photos, she thought of the murder weapon. A nylon cord like that could easily be used in a magic show, maybe as one of the many straps of a straightjacket.

As she searched the files, Jordan gave a faint smile. "Told you it would be a him."

Maeve returned the smile, feeling a sense of determination wash over her.

“Maybe statistics were right this time.”

“Always are,” he said.

They could do this.

They *had* to do this.

Failure was not an option.

She moved the files, satisfied that they had enough to go on to pick the guy up. She got her computer, and then, on the Artful Dodger's website, found that he had a show that night. It started in half an hour.

She slammed the laptop closed and almost sprinted out of the offices, grabbing Jordan’s car keys.

"Come on!" she urged, while he was still on the phone with forensics, waving the keys in his face. "We have to get to him before his show starts.”

Jordan didn't wait for any more explanation.

He quickly ended the call with forensics and followed Maeve out of the building. They hurried to the parking lot and jumped into Jordan's car. Maeve gave him the address of the theater where the Artful Dodger's show was being held, and Jordan revved the engine, speeding off towards their destination.

"Forensics says that they don't have a record of his DNA. Once we get that, we'll be able to know if he was at any of the crime scenes."

"Good." Maeve said. They were getting close. She could feel it. "What's his real name?"

"It's Nick. Nick Stephenson."

***

The two detectives arrived at the show's venue just minutes before the Artful Dodger was set to be on stage. Maeve and Jordan pushed through the crowd of expectant people to the ticketing desk.

"We have to be let through to see Nick Stephenson," said Maeve, with all the urgency in her voice.

"Do you have a VIP backstage ticket?" said the woman, who sat slumped over the desk, wearing a scarlet blazer and a frown.

"I'll do you one better," Jordan said, showing her his badge.

The woman simply sighed and rolled her eyes. "I guess that's good enough. Come on. This way."

She handed the two over to a security officer, who showed them through the halls of the stage, past the theater of red-upholstered seats, and into the main dressing room.

The room itself was huge—decked out with blue velvet drapes and even a gold-trimmed mini bar. Framed pictures of the venue's most iconic performers covered the wall, other escape artists, magicians, and singers.

The room was also more crowded than Maeve thought it would be. Backstage VIPs, people who worked with the venue, a publicist, a makeup artist, someone in charge of the wardrobe, were all crowded around Nick.

"Now remember, the oxygen tank is under your right sleeve," one of them said, as he slid on his costume.

"You can't be back here," another one of them said to the two detectives, undoubtedly his agent.

But Maeve showed him her badge and explained the situation.

As she crossed the room, she looked at one of the straightjackets used in his act, with sleeves that buckled to each other with a long nylon strap. Only on this straightjacket, the strap had been cut off.

The Artful Dodger was standing in front of the mirror, with his back to them. He was dressed in a black leather jacket, with a white shirt and black jeans.

Maeve's heart was pounding in her chest as she approached him.

"Nick Stephenson?" she said.

The Artful Dodger spun around on his heels, and Maeve felt a jolt of recognition. The lower half of his face was exactly what she had seen in the photo and in the flier— a chiseled jaw. He had thick dark hair and mischievous eyes, and his build was muscular but agile.

"What's going on?" he asked, an edge to his voice.

One of the stage assistants flocked to his side, gently grabbing his arm.

"We need to ask you some questions in connection to an investigation," Maeve explained.

"This is ridiculous," said a woman, approaching from the corner of the room. She was in a sequined dress that complemented Nick's ensemble. She must have been a stage assistant.

"Nick needs to get ready to go on stage," she insisted.

"What was the nature of your relationship with Juliette Cavendish, Emily Smith, and Adrienne Howe?" Maeve said, ignoring any protests from the assistant or the agent.

Maybe it was a little rushed to ask such questions right away.

But it was the only way to get his full attention.

Maeve waited for him to get defensive, maybe even run away, but he didn't.

Instead, he sighed.

"I knew this was coming," he said.

"Don't say that, Nick," the assistant said, a commanding tone in her voice.

"Nick, they haven't charged you with anything, she said.

Then the agent stepped forward again. "You need to be on stage in two minutes." He shot Maeve a sharp look. "I don't know what exactly it is that you think you're doing here, but Nick has a very important show. Perhaps if you come back with some kind of warrant..."

"Drew, no, it's okay," Nick said, as he ran a nervous hand over his hair. "I suppose all secrets have to come out eventually, don't they?"

And then he looked at Maeve, almost sorrowfully.

"Then you won't mind coming along and answering a few more questions for us, would you, Nick?" she asked.

He shook his head. "If that's what you need from me. I'll have to cancel the show, but..."

Jordan already had him in handcuffs. "Standard procedure," he explained.

"Do what you have to do," Nick agreed. “But trust me, they won’t do you much good.”

The two walked him back down the hall, past the line of people all taking photos of him on their phones. They were followed by hundreds of eyes, and questions. "What is going on? where are they taking him?"

Nick went willingly into the back of Jordan's car.

Something unsettled Maeve as she pushed through the growing crowd of people to get into the passenger’s seat.

Why was Nick so willing?

Did he want them to catch him?

CHAPTER TWENTY TWO

Since they were too far from the field office, Maeve took their new suspect to a nearby LVMPD precinct, the one that had initially reported the case. Once they were inside, Maeve led Nick into an interrogation room, while Jordan followed behind.

The room inside was cold and stark, the concrete floor and white walls not offering any warmth or comfort. The only thing in here was a black, steel table with a bolted down chair. A single fluorescent bulb hung in the center of the ceiling. The whole building had the smell of Windex and bleach, as the janitor had just finished his shift, cleaning blood and grime out of the precinct.

The room was quiet, save for a ticking clock.

Maeve's tongue felt dry, like there was a ball of cotton in her mouth.

Maeve turned to her laptop and began to sift through the case files again. She read over the witness statements, the forensic reports, everything. She wanted to go into the interrogation prepared.

"What's the plan?" Jordan asked, appearing next to her with a cup of coffee in his hand.

On the other side of the glass, Nick looked resigned, calm, disheartened. He leaned over the table with folded arms.

"I already asked local police to check his show schedule on the night of the three murders. But right now, he doesn't seem to have an alibi."

Jordan nodded and took a tentative sip of his coffee. “Would it kill LVMPD to get a better coffee maker?”

“Focus, please,” Maeve said.

“Hey, I haven’t slept in two days.”

"He wasn't very concerned when he canceled that show," Maeve continued, trying not to feel too sorry for him. "How much money do you think he'll lose for it?"

"No idea," Jordan said with a shrug. "I'm not sure what's going on in his head."

"Let's start with the basics," Maeve said, opening a file as they entered the room. "Can you confirm that you are Nick Stephenson?"

"Yes, I am," Nick said.

"And you perform under the name, the Artful Dodger?"

Nick nodded. "Yes, that's correct."

Maeve took a deep breath, then leaned forward. "Nick, we need to talk about the murders of Juliette Cavendish, Emily Smith, and Adrienne Howe."

Nick's demeanor changed at the mention of their names. He looked down at the table, his face creasing in pain.

"Can you tell us more about your relationship to the three victims?"

Nick's shoulders slumped, and he took a deep breath. "I knew them all," he admitted. "I met them all through my shows. They were fans."

Nick looked up, his eyes searching Maeve's face before settling on a spot behind her. "I was... involved with all three of them," he said quietly. "I know it looks bad, but I had nothing to do with their deaths."

Maeve noticed the way his hands were shaking, the way he couldn't quite meet her gaze.

She almost couldn't believe what she was hearing.

Selina's lead had been right.

"Tell me about your relationships with them," she urged gently.

"Juliette, I met her first. We got drinks after one of my shows, and something about her was just so special. My dad was a bit of an asshole too so we bonded over that. But it was over quickly. I mean, she was just so... high maintenance."

Maeve frowned at how casually he had tossed Juliette aside. For all her drama, Juliette seemed to have been a nice girl under it all.

"Emily... she was too obsessed with me. She used to check my phone when we were together. Told me that I couldn't text anyone else. Not even my stage assistant. Anyway, that ended pretty quickly."

He ran a nervous hand through his hair.

"Adrienne was just a fling. Only a couple of nights. Out-of-towners, you know?"

"Did you have access to any of their hotel rooms?" Jordan asked.

Nick sighed. "I did. I won't try to hide it. You'll probably find my fingerprints all over all three rooms. Juliette gave me a key card almost immediately. I knew exactly how to get to Emily's room. They always opened the door when I knocked."

"Why did you break it off with these women?" Maeve asked. "Did they find out you were cheating?"

"Cheating? No. I would never do that. I know this whole story makes me seem like a dirtbag, but I'm not. I promise. I just... it started when Juliette saw me backstage before one of my shows. I caught her taking pictures of a set piece in my act. If my competitors ever saw that... if the media did..."

Maeve looked over at Jordan. Could finding out a secret about his act really be worth killing someone?

But then again, magicians like him took their craft seriously. His entire livelihood, his entire future, depended on his ability to protect the secrets of how he escaped elaborate designed cages, water tanks, and straightjackets.

Information leaking about how he did it could end him.

"Emily found out something when she was searching through my phone too," he said. "I know I have to be more careful."

“Did all three of them find out a secret into your escapes on stage?” Maeve asked.

That kind of information could be worth a lot to the right reporter, blogger, or curious fan.

He sighed, and then nodded slowly.

Maeve frowned. He had a clear motive, clear opportunity.

"And where were you on the nights of each murder?" Maeve asked.

He fidgeted in his chair. "Nowhere. Some of the few nights I stayed home alone. I get really tired after my shows. I just need a night to myself every once and a while.”

Maeve stared at him for a long moment. He had all but admitted to killing these three women.

He fit the profile perfectly.

So perfectly, that almost no other suspect in any other case she had worked had been this clearly guilty.

She could already see him at his court date. He was the type to try to garner sympathy from the jury with puppy dog eyes. But his cheap tricks and gimmicks wouldn't help him in a real prison, or against a good prosecutor. Whatever genuine skill he had to open locks and escape would be useless against the armored doors and security cameras of prison.

Maeve got ready to leave the room, but Nick looked heartbroken, almost about to cry.

“I didn't do it," he said, his voice barely above a whisper. "I know that doesn't mean much, coming from me," he said. "I know that I don't have an alibi, and that I look super guilty. But for what it's worth, I didn't do it."

Maeve leaned forward over the table and looked him in the eye.

"I'd rethink my legal strategy, if I were you. You'll get a shorter sentence if you plead guilty."

***

Jordan shot Maeve a concerned look once the door to the interrogation room was closed, and Nick could no longer see them. He gave a deep sigh.

“Well,” he said. “I don’t know what more we could ask for.”.

Maeve nodded.

But as she looked back at the suspect through the glass, she wondered.

Had this been too easy?

“Oh no,” Jordan said. “You have that look on your face.”

“What look on my face?”

“You have your ‘something doesn’t add up’ look on your face.”

"Doesn’t it all feel a little circumstantial to you?" she asked, crossing her arms.

“Did you hear yourself in there?” he responded, gesturing to the window.

“He had every reason to lie. To make up an alibi to waste our time, dig his heels in about knowing the three victims… but he didn’t.”

"It's a tactic," Jordan said. "He knows his lies won't hold up, so he's trying to get us to feel bad for him."

"Maybe," Maeve answered, but she didn't sound convinced.

"Detective Sharp!" said a voice from behind them. A uniformed police officer approached from around the corner. "There's a phone call for you," she said, holding up one of the precinct’s phones.

Maeve frowned, wondering who could be calling her at this hour. She took the phone from the officer and answered, "Detective Sharp speaking."

"Ms. Sharp. I heard you made the arrest. Congratulations."

"Who is this?" she asked, a feeling of concern creeping up her throat.

"You don't remember? This is Kirk Cavendish. You're a detective, you should probably recognize people's voices."

"Hello, Mr. Cavendish," she replied. The hair on her arms stood on end at the thought of the man. His voice sounded slippery; he was a little too pleased.

"Should have known it would be one of those half-rate charlatan bastards. The city's just crawling with them."

Maeve bit her lip. "You should know that we're questioning a suspect at this time. No official arrest has been made yet."

There was a long, cold pause on the other end. "Why not? From what I hear, this is open and shut. You have enough on this guy to put him away for what he did to me. Me and my business."

Maeve swayed back and forth, trying not to feel too frustrated with this man.

"Everyone deserves due process," she said. "We have to examine every possibility. All the details surrounding the case are confidential," said Maeve. "How did you know about any of this?"

"I have some valuable sources," he said, with a sly tone in his voice.

"We're working as fast as we can, Mr. Cavendish, but I want this case to be air tight. I'd rather take my time now than risk the suspect walking free if he's really guilty."

"You let me think about juries," he said.

Maeve was becoming more and more concerned with Cavendish by the second. He couldn't really swing a jury, could he?

"Just remember, Ms. Sharp, that you're not just catching a serial killer. You're catching the man who took my daughter from me, at great risk to my business. There are higher stakes to this than just one half-rate con-artist getting away. Don't do something you'll regret."

And then the line went dead.

"What was that about?" asked Jordan.

"Mr. Cavendish really wants us to make an arrest. He thinks this is the best outcome for the case."

"Ten second ago, you agreed with him," Jordan said. "What changed?"

Maeve couldn't answer. There was still one thought gnawing at the back of her mind.

He had everything to gain by lying.

But instead, he chose to tell the truth.

Why?

Unless he was innocent…

Before she could try to explain this to Jordan, another woman stormed through the front doors of the precinct. Maeve recognized her as the assistant in his act.

"I have to see him!" she said, almost in a scream. Mascara ran down her face, and she stumbled in her high heels, still wearing her glittering show dress.

Maeve quickly moved towards her, placing a hand on her shoulder. "Ma'am, who do you need to see?"

"Nick," the assistant breathed out. "I need to talk to Nick. He's innocent."

Jordan raised an eyebrow, and Maeve motioned for him to follow her as they led the assistant to an empty room.

"What makes you think he's innocent?" Maeve asked softly. If she could calm her down, then maybe she could get some good information from her.

"He's not capable of doing something like this." she shook her head and wiped her running nose. "I know him better than anyone. He's a kind person, generous to a fault. He would never hurt anyone, let alone murder three women. You have to let me in to see him. Please?"

"It goes against procedure," said Jordan.

She looked completely distraught. "I have to talk to him. Just for five minutes?"

"What's your name, ma'am?" asked Jordan.

"Vivian. My name is Vivian Hargrove."

Maeve signed. She was so tired, and she just wanted the case to be done. It wasn't exactly protocol to let friends in.

"Please?" she said again. "I know it doesn't look like it, but I actually have a law degree. I just want to help Nick out. He doesn't have a lawyer."

"Fine," Maeve said, knowing that refusing her could open her up to serious consequences. "But only for a few minutes."

When they stopped outside the room, she looked up at Maeve.

"You'll turn off the microphone, right? It's just I think you could get into a lot of trouble if he was being listened to and didn't know it."

Maeve didn't like the idea of not being able to hear what was going on in that room, but she knew that Vivian was right.

Jordan unlocked the door for her while Maeve switched off the microphone and tape. They wouldn't be able to hear anything that happened next.

CHAPTER TWENTY THREE

Vivian's tears were gone by the time the door slammed shut behind her.

Nick was a sight—sitting there with his head in his hands, hunched over like he was the one who had been through the ringer. He looked pale and gaunt, with dark circles under his eyes. But, despite everything, he looked up and smiled when he saw Vivian come in.

The law degree had been an easy lie to get her in the door.

She wanted to let herself smile at it all, at how well her plan was going, but she kept her composure calm. She thought back to the years they had spent together working on their act. In their college days, Nick had been so different. He lacked the confidence of the award-winning performer that he had become. He was just a scrawny kid, with a fascination with locks, With ridiculous dreams of becoming the world's greatest escape artist.

That was how they'd met—he was sitting in the quad of their alma mater, holding a pair of handcuffs, and he stopped her and asked her if she would cuff them behind his back.

"I need to practice." he said, showing her the unfolded paper clip buried in the soft part of his palm. And she had been shocked but fascinated, and she watched him struggle for thirty minutes. She told him she would unlock him if he wanted her to, but every time he refused.

"How will I learn?" he told her.

When he finally opened the handcuffs, he introduced himself.

As the two became friends, he taught her the beginnings of what it took to become an escape artist, but she taught herself the rest, reading old books on the greats—Houdini, Saltini, anyone at all.

And when she got better than Nick, no one noticed.

"Our act." That is what the two called it when they built it together. When they spent years hand-making cages with false backs, unnoticeable oxygen tanks, straightjackets you could worm your way out of.

Our act. That is what they called it when the two friends drove to Vegas together with all their earthly belongings in the trunk of the car.

Somewhere along the rise to fame, for Nick, it became, "My act." There wasn't one escape he did that she didn't help create. The best parts of the show had been her idea entirely.

But Nick seemed to forget about this: when the women started knocking on his door after every show, when the paparazzi only ever looked at him. When he got sloppy, it almost cost everyone involved their whole careers because he couldn't keep a secret.

He had been so eager to show off to each woman who gave him the slightest bit of attention.

"We're best friends, aren't we, Viv?" he used to say. He said it before leaving for Emily's, and then she was the one he came back and complained to. She was the one he told when Juliette dumped him, she was the one who hugged him, stroked his hair, and told him everything was going to be alright.

But then he sold the rights to the show—her show-—to a huge theater company. There would be 100 Artful Dodgers all over the United States, playing private clubs and small theaters. Nick had trademarked the name, and Vivian wouldn't see a penny of the profits.

"Do you think I made the right decision?" he asked her, just a few weeks before that moment.

She had told him that of course he had.

Because Nick had never been able to handle the truth.

Standing in that interrogation room, she saw for the first time how small he was. She had loved him once, she realized. But that time had long passed.

"Hey," he said. "What are you doing here?"

Vivian moved closer to him, taking his hand in hers. She had to have his trust if the final part of her plan was to work. She could pretend—she had been doing it for over a decade while they worked together.

"I had to see you," she said. "Nick, I know you didn't do this."

"I think you're the only one, Viv," he said.

That was so like him, to lead her on, make her feel like she was the only thing that mattered, when really, he just talked that way to keep people loyal to him.

"I think you might be right," she said. She turned the tears back on for his benefit. Mustering them was easy. All she had to do was think of the years of heartbreak and betrayal.

"I've been thinking, Nick," she said. "I heard them talking in the hallway. They're going to arrest you."

"I know," he said, burying his head in his hands. "I'll just have to hope that with a good lawyer, I can put this all behind me."

Even now, he was too dense to understand.

"A good lawyer?" she said. "Nick, you're an escape artist for crying out loud. The fact that you've willingly stayed here for so long..."

"There's nothing I can do, Viv."

But she knew for a fact that the great Artful Dodger kept a paperclip up his sleeve at all times.

This seemed to impress fans when he met them, but Vivian had always seen it as an endearing old habit that he had yet to leave behind him, with his days of bar magic and picking open handcuffs. All she had to do was convince him to use it.

"I don't know what you think a lawyer is going to do for you," she said. "You don't have an alibi. You have means and motive. It doesn't look good. Even to a jury that's already inclined to like you."

"I don't know what else to say, Viv," he said, getting frustrated. "All I have is the truth. That will be enough."

"No. It won't." She leaned forward, bringing her face close to his, and whispered, "Did you know that Nevada serves the death penalty? If you plead innocent, you'll definitely get it. If you plead guilty for a reduced sentence, then you'll spend the rest of your life in jail. How much do you think your little paperclip is going to help you out in there, huh?"

She watched the color melt from his face.

Vivian leaned back against the wall, and crossed her arms. She had him now.

"But this place on the other hand..." she looked from one side of the room to the other. "I've seen you bust out of this kind of place thousands of times."

He picked at his fingernails, as he always did when he was nervous. She could tell he was cracking, ready to do whatever she said.

"Come find me in a few hours," she said. "Make sure you change clothes before then so you're not seen. I'll help you disappear."

"Disappear?"

For her, this meant another rope around his neck. It would look like a suicide.

The cops would prefer it that way, to end with a nice, neat closure. The news would say that the Artful Dodger, after killing three women and escaping custody, realized that he couldn't outrun the law, and decided to end it all on his own terms.

Vivian already had the note written up.

But she would make sure he knew it was her. That after all he had taken from her, he would look her in the eye.

"I have some money saved," is what she said out loud. "You could go somewhere else. Somewhere far away. Start over. You could get a new identity."

"I wouldn't be able to perform--"

"Who gives a shit?" she said. "We're talking about your life here. As if they'd let you perform in prison."

He shook his head.

"I just don't..."

"Look at me, Nick," she said. She stepped forward and lifted his face towards her. "There isn't any other option. I'm sorry."

After a long pause, he nodded. "Okay."

"Okay," she echoed. "Everything will work out. I promise. Meet me behind the old theater tonight. Three hours."

He nodded again.

There was a knock on the door, and from the other side, one of the detectives said, "That's five minutes."

She left, with tears still in her eyes.

"I just can't believe it..." she said, as she emerged from the room. "I can't believe this could happen to someone like him... but you're right. He told me about all the evidence you have. He still says he didn't do it but I just can't deny..."

The detective ate it up. He placed a comforting hand on her shoulder, and said, "People are surprising. Anyone can turn to killing, if pushed to their limits."

She smirked. "I guess so."

As she left the precinct, she thought about what would happen after her plan finally worked out. The deal to expand the Artful Dodger's show would of course be void. It would be in bad taste, after all, and his name would forever be sullied. The only other person who knew how to carry out his act was Vivian herself.

She could already see her name in lights above all the major venues.

The Vanishing Vivian.

For a change, everyone would be looking at her.

CHAPTER TWENTY FOUR

Maeve watched Nick's assistant leave. There was an energy with which she walked, almost glee, as she left the precinct, almost as though she was excited. Something about her body language didn't feel right to Maeve. She hadn't been able to hear anything that she said to Nick in the interrogation room, but she could see the two of them together through the reflective glass.

There was something strange in the way she'd reached forward and lifted his face up to hers.

But as far as Maeve could see, the case was over. Nick admitted to all their suspicions—even the fact that he had access to all the hotel rooms. Once all the warrants went through, he would be charged within the hour.

Sure, they didn't have a confession. But you didn't need one in the presence of such good evidence—DNA, opportunity, motive.

Jordan returned after walking Vivian out the door. The two stood in the middle of the precinct's kitchen, next to an ancient-looking coffee maker and fridge that looked as if it had seen better days.

"She's distraught," he said. "I guess it sucks to find out that the people closest to you aren't who you think they are."

"I know," Maeve said, thinking of Nick himself.

Could a man like that really be honest?

A lifetime of performance, of lying to the crowds, night after night. Such a life would teach you how to become the most convincing liar. You'd be able to look an FBI detective in the eye, with all the sorrow in the world, and say, "I didn't do it."

But some small part of her wasn't satisfied.

What if somehow he was telling the truth?

But that was impossible… it couldn't be.

Jordan broke her from her trance. "Hey, let me buy you a beer for a job well done," he offered.

Maeve smiled and checked her watch. She needed a drink after the long day, and the looming sense of unease that still lingered.

"Do you think he did it?" she asked.

"A little late to be asking, don't you think?"

Maeve shrugged. "I mean, it's not our place to say, right? Just to present the evidence, and the jury will make the call?"

"Lighten up, Sharp. You caught the guy."

Maeve nodded, but her mind was still racing. She couldn't shake the feeling that something was off. She wanted to believe that Nick was being honest. And the way Nick had looked at her, like she held all the answers, like he was relying on her to get him out.

As Maeve put on her coat, Jordan stood behind her, impatiently awaiting a much-needed break from police work.

"I've got to say," he began. "I'm impressed. First case on the job, and you've closed in no time. This city has the tendency to chew people up and spit them back out, but it doesn't seem to do that to you."

"Maybe you just don't know me well enough yet," said Maeve.

"Good job, is all I'm saying. I've worked on a lot of cases. But I've never worked with anyone who could solve one like you."

Maeve felt her cheeks go hot. Was she blushing?

"Are you being... *nice*... to me, Detective?"

He held up his hands defensively. "Sorry, sorry. Won't happen again."

For the first time in weeks, Maeve laughed.

But even as they were halfway out the door, on their way to the nearest bar, Maeve couldn't shake the feeling that something was off. Maybe it was nothing... but maybe it wasn't.

Years on the job taught you to hone your instincts. And Maeve never doubted hers.

"The other agents love to go to this bar," he said.

She got into his car, and tried to focus as he pulled down the road.

"What's you're drink of choice? You strike me as a red wine kind of person."

"I'm going to try to not be insulted by that," she said.

A few minutes later, the two went to this famous bar, filled with law enforcement off duty. Jordan found the two of them a small table in the corner, and he drank a beer while she sipped tentatively at an old fashioned.

"What's wrong?" he asked, noticing how quiet she had gotten.

"Did you see Vivian when she left after speaking to Nick? She seemed so happy, almost like she knew something no one else did."

"Okay..." he said slowly. "Sharp, we've almost closed the case. Take the win."

"Her body language too… like she was going somewhere. And it seemed really strange when she was talking to him. Something isn't right."

Jordan gave a reluctant sigh. "You want to go back and check on him, don't you?"

"No," she said, taking another half-sip of her drink.

Jordan raised an eyebrow.

"Yes."

"Fine," he said, swiping his keys off the table. "Good thing we weren't here that long, and I can still drive."

Maeve tapped her foot the whole car ride back to the field office, waiting in anticipation to find out what didn't sit right with her.

"It's probably nothing," she said to herself and to Jordan, over and over again.

When the car finally got back to the parking lot, she didn't wait for Jordan to park. She sprinted out and jogged back to the building, past a group of confused-looking officers. She walked as fast as she could back up the hall to the interrogation rooms.

"What's going on?" one of the officers asked, as she sped past the bullpen.

"It's nothing," Maeve assured her. She could feel sweat beading on her forehead as she ran down the hall. Her heart beat in her ears.

She rounded the corner to the interrogation room, and through the one way glass…

Nothing.

Nick was gone.

The only thing that remained was an unlocked pair of handcuffs on the table.

"Shit!" Maeve burst through the door, even though she knew that no one was hiding on the other side. Nick had vanished into thin air, without a trace that he had ever been there.

Jordan appeared a few moments later, car keys still in his hand, and stared wide-eyed at the empty room.

"But I–" he began.

"Why didn't we put extra security on the escape artist?" Maeve said, furious with herself that she hadn't suggested it.

"He seemed so compliant," said Jordan.

But Maeve didn't hear him. She was too busy getting the whole precinct into lockdown.

She sprinted into the hall and found the officer who had asked her if everyone was alright. "The suspect has escaped," she said. "No one gets in or out of this building, do you understand? Seal all the doors, make sure that there is an officer posted at each one of them."

"Yes, ma'am," the officer said, running towards the captain's office.

Maeve couldn't believe it. How had she missed this?

Did Vivian help him escape? Even if she did, it wouldn't have been hard. All it would have taken was to get out of the handcuffs, then out of the locked door. Beyond that, there were dozens of entrances, exits, and fire escapes to choose from.

"Set up a five-block perimeter around the building," she yelled to the lieutenant, standing at the ready. "He can't have gotten far."

The lockdown alarm blared in her ears as Maeve sprinted to the nearest exit to look for him herself. She showed the officer guarding the door her badge, and Jordan followed close behind.

Dozens of officers, all covered in bullet-proof vests followed after her, carrying flashlights, getting into squad cars.

"Put out an APB," she told one of them, and she scanned the outside of the building.

It didn't make sense. Even if he could pick the locks to his handcuffs and the door to the interrogation room, how could he have slipped past so many cops undetected? Surely one of them would have recognized him as the suspect they were holding in the interrogation room.

Unless…

Maeve walked to the far side of the building, where there was a window, not far from the interrogation room.

And when Maeve looked at it from outside, it was wide open.

He must have slipped down the hallway unnoticed, opened the window, and climbed down the brick wall, clinging to the tiny cracks and outcroppings of stone. She suspected that the security cameras would show as much.

From there, he only had to run through the network of dark alleys to freedom.

How long had he been gone? If it had been since Vivian left, then he was long-past their five-block perimeter, on his way into hiding, where they might never find him.

Jordan found her outside. She was still muttering to herself about APBs, perimeters, and open windows.

"They've searched the whole building. He's long gone," Jordan said, putting a hand on her shoulder.

Maeve looked up at him, the realization of what had just happened slowly sinking in. She had known that something was wrong, but she had let Vivian's presence distract her from making sure that Nick was securely detained. More than that, she had so badly wanted to believe him that she didn't register him as a threat. She chose to believe the lie of innocence that he crafted.

"I can't believe I missed it," she said, her voice barely above a whisper.

"It's not your fault," Jordan said. "We all missed it. We'll get him, Maeve. We'll find him."

Maeve shook her head. "Where could he have gone? He's too smart to go back to his apartment. He can't go back to the venue. Tell someone to put a block on his passport."

"Already done," said Jordan.

Maeve racked her brain, trying to think of any possible places that Nick could hide. He was a smart man, and he wouldn't have left any clues behind. She worried that the police would search the streets all night, but there were a thousand possible ways to slip through their defenses, and only so many officers to do the job. By morning, he could be on his way to Mexico or finding his way across the country to forge a new identity.

"Wait a minute," Maeve said, suddenly remembering something. "Vivian. We need to bring her in for questioning again."

"One thing at a time," Jordan said. "You know this city. You want to go somewhere where no one will see you, where do you go?"

Maeve shrugged. "Honestly, the strip. It's easiest to hide in a crowd."

Jordan shook his head. "He's too popular for that. Too high profile. He's not going to risk getting recognized."

Maeve racked her brain for more places. She had spent most of her time in the suburbs with her family. By the time she started investigating crime, she had left Vegas far behind.

"What about that abandoned theater?" Jordan suggested. "You know the one… it's north of here. It's secluded. It's dark. It's always half under refurbishment, so it's got plenty of cover. He could meet up there with Vivian if she is helping him escape. It's the only place in the city that fits the profile."

"It's not the only abandoned building in the area."

"I was there for a drug bust recently," he reassured her. "No one does *anything* legal there."

Of course, Maeve remembered the abandoned building, pushed back from the strip. The place had always creeped her out as a child, with its missing letters on the sign out front and the chain link fence that surrounded the whole property. But it was just the kind of place that an escape artist on the run would go.

"Come on Maeve, you trust your instincts. I trust mine," he pushed.

She didn't like how shaky it was, but it was the only idea they had.

"We'll ask local police to send uniformed officers to other hideouts in the area, and we'll check that one first."

CHAPTER TWENTY FIVE

Vivian waited in the abandoned theater. The venue was a relic of a bygone era, located on a seedy street on the outskirts of Las Vegas. The once-grand building had seen better days, with its faded paint, cracked plaster, and broken windows. Ivy had grown up on the sides of the walls, reaching up towards the sky as if in a desperate attempt to escape the decaying building.

Inside, the air was thick with dust and the smell of rot. The seats were torn and frayed, and the stage was littered with broken props and forgotten costumes. The curtains were threadbare, hanging limply from their rods, and the only light came from a few dim bulbs that flickered overhead.

Outside, the once-great theater's name was etched in fading letters: The Rialto.

Sometimes Vivian would come here to think, when she needed to get away from the continuous crowd of the city, or when she needed inspiration for a new act.

It had been a wonderful part of the city a hundred years ago, but when an escape artist died on stage—drowned in a tank of water that he couldn't escape from fast enough—the theater company was put under review. Eventually, the scandal put them out of business, and the place changed hands a few times before being seized by the city when they discovered it was being used as a front for money laundering.

Maybe it was the rumors of the escape artist’s ghost walking on the stage, or the myth that you could still find blood money tucked into the walls, but the lot had been for sale for as long as anyone could remember.

It was filled with old scaffolding and supplies to repair it, but each attempt at refurbishing it to its old glory had been abandoned, along with the rest of the building.

Now it was used for things that people didn't want to be seen—shady deals, fornication, and... if the time was right... murder.

As Vivian waited, she became impatient.

How long did it take one man to walk to the north side of the city? Vivian was long past remorse. She knew she couldn't sugar coat what she was really doing to Nick.

Nick had been her best friend. She'd even thought he could be the love of her life. Once.

Now he was just a painful memory.

He had changed too much since she met him that day on the quad in college.

Maybe she would buy the Rialto, with the money she got when she took over his act. It had to pay much better than just being the lowly stage assistant. In a few years, she'd have enough money to start her own theater company, refurbish this old theater for good.

The rumors of the haunted halls would be a selling point for the right crowd.

Of course, by then, there would be one more rumor associated with those historic walls.

The suicide of Nick Stephenson. The once-great escape artist.

She waited with a sturdy rope she'd bought earlier that day. After it was done, she'd swing him from the rafters for good measure, then sanitize the place, erasing any evidence that she ever set foot on the grounds.

When the police found him, there would be only one conclusion to draw— Nick escaped custody but had nowhere else to turn, and in one last desperate attempt to escape, hung himself.

It was the perfect plan.

Finally, the old front doors creaked open, and Nick walked in. His gate was slow, his shoulders were slumped.

"Vivian," he said, in a tired voice, that she had heard thousands of times before.

For a moment she felt a surge of relief.

But it quickly turned to dread as she looked at him, seeing the weariness and desperation etched into his features. But she strengthened her resolve. She had done this before, after all, and there was no turning back now.

Those other women—they had been a means to an end. But she would have to look Nick in the eye, thinking of all the things they had been through together while she watched the light fade from his face.

She knew what she had to do… but this felt different.

She would have to be stronger than before.

In a way, it was strangely satisfying to know that she would be with Nick in his last moments. Even though it had to end this way, she would still be there for him, through the terror of it.

"What's wrong?" she asked, trying to keep her voice steady.

"I don't know about all this, Viv. Starting over? I don't know if I can do it."

"Of course you can," she said, with a sing-song voice, waiting for him to come close enough. She'd already tied the hangman's noose. She just needed to get close enough to him to use it.

Nick took a step closer, and Vivian could see the desperation in his eyes. He hadn't changed his clothes like she'd told him to.

"I mean it, Vivian. This isn't what I signed up for. It's... it's too much."

She took another step closer, her heart pounding in her chest. The moment of truth was here. She raised her hand to his face, her fingers brushing lightly against his cheek.

"It'll be okay, Nick," she cooed. "We'll make it through this together."

He nodded reluctantly.

"I know you didn't do this, Nick, but to those dumb cops, it looks bad. The nylon used to kill them looks just like the straps on the straightjacket you use in your act. And one of them is missing. This is the only choice you have."

Vivian was about to loop the rope around his neck, but a strange look appeared on his face as she said this. Almost confused. He knit his brow.

"Wait a second..." he began, stepping away, just out of reach.

"How did you know that?"

"How did I know what?" she answered, as innocently as she could.

"The details of the case. The cops didn't tell anyone. They didn't tell anyone that they found my prints in all three hotel rooms."

"What do you mean?" she asked again. If she could get him talking for long enough, then she could sneak closer, shortening the distance between them. But he kept walking backwards, slipping farther and farther from her reach.

It was only a matter of time, after all, before he noticed the noose in her hand.

"I mean that you shouldn't know about that," Nick said, his voice shaking.

Vivian's heart sank. This was not how she had planned it. She had thought that she could easily manipulate Nick into believing that this was the only way out for him. But now, he was catching on.

"How could you have known about the murder weapon?" he asked. “The FBI kept that confidential.”

Vivian stole another step closer.

"Unless..."

"Unless what?" she said, her tone turning sharper with every moment.

"Unless you had something to do with it."

She pursed her lips. "You're not being serious, are you?"

"You were the only other person in the world who knew that I saw those three women. Hell, I even told you where their hotel rooms were... you weren't... *jealous*... were you?"

Vivian felt the panic creeping in. This was not how it was supposed to go. She had planned everything down to the smallest detail, but she hadn't accounted for Nick's suspicion. In her mind, he went to her willingly, and maybe even confessed how she had been the one he had really loved all this time. And she would look him in the eye, wipe his tears, and tell him it was too late.

In her mind, he accepted it all with understanding. Knowing the inevitability. He would apologize, and she would have the joy of not accepting it.

"You're being paranoid," she said, taking a step forward. "I would never hurt you, Nick. You're my friend."

Nick backed away, his eyes darting around the room. "You're the one who told me to escape. We don't know what would have happened if I had stayed, but now I've broken the law for real."

"Nick..." she began.

"I don't know what to believe anymore. All I know is that I need to get out of here."

He turned and made a run for the door, but Vivian was faster.

She lurched for him, and wrapped the rope around his neck.

The shock of it sent him tumbling to the ground. He hit the theater's old floorboards with a resounding thud. His hands shot to his throat, but Vivian walked back too quickly, allowing the knot to tighten.

"You were always so oblivious, Nick," she said.

"Please--" he choked out, pulling at the rope, trying to breathe.

"Jealous of them? Jealous of you? You were always so oblivious, do you know that? Did you ever think about how you took our show, the one we built together, and you got all the attention, and the fame, and the credit, while I was just eye candy on stage right. Night after night... I watched you preen for the world, and then you ignored me. I was your friend, I was your best friend. And maybe I did love you... in some way. At one time."

She was pulling the rope hard now, so hard that she dragged his body back through the dust. His face was turning from red to purple, but he still tried desperately to gasp in what little air he could.

"You killed those women, Nick. *You* killed them the moment you got involved with them."

But she stopped walking, and the rope went slack. Nick used this moment to slip his hands under the rope, loosen the noose, and slip free.

"No!" she screamed.

He raced to the door, but she was faster, blocking his only exit, forcing him to turn away, deeper into the theater.

Vivian doubled back towards the stage, where she took an old piece of chair leg, heavy and rusted. She couldn't catch him with a few feet of rope, but if she incapacitated him, she could still reasonably make it look like suicide.

"You can't run from what you've done to me," she yelled, her voice echoing through the empty rafters. "Not anymore."

And she took off after him, into the darkness of the theater.

CHAPTER TWENTY SIX

Jordan's car sped into the crumbling circular drive that led up to the building. Maeve looked up at the theater, with a few lights on in the upper rooms. Other than that, it looked completely abandoned, with peeling paint and termite-eaten walls.

"I'm impressed you thought of this place," Maeve said. She checked that her gun was still loaded, before stepping out of the car.

"Busted some drug dealers here a few weeks ago. Did you know, there's this rumor, that the ghost of an escape artist still wanders..."

"Another time, maybe?" Maeve suggested, with a tense smile.

"Right."

She shrugged into her bullet-proof vest, and Jordan did the same.

"Should we have called for backup before coming here?" Jordan asked.

Maeve shook her head. "If we're wrong, then we need as many officers as we can get searching the streets. The wider the net we cast, the more likely it is that we will find him."

"And if he is here..." said Jordan. "And he's armed and dangerous?"

"Then we deal with it," Maeve replied.

"So, what's the plan?".

"Okay," she said, gathering her thoughts. She tucked her hair behind her ears so it would stay out of her way. "You're right that we don't know the situation in there. But we have reason to believe that Nick Stephenson is a dangerous fugitive. He's running from three counts of murder in the first degree. We have to assume that he's armed and dangerous. I think that we should proceed with caution."

"But still no backup?"

Maeve reconsidered for a moment.

"If we wait too long, he could escape out the back before we have a chance to catch him. We're just two people, we can't secure the perimeter of the building reliably enough."

Jordan nodded. "So we go in."

"If we don't, we risk losing him for good."

"I'm in," said Jordan, loading his gun.

Maeve slowly crossed the front of the property, littered with cigarette butts and broken glass. The closer she got, the more her heart raced in her chest, but she did her best to appear calm and composed. She led the way up the stairs to the front entrance of the building. There was a wide array of long-burned light bulbs overhead and fogged glass doors in front of her.

She placed a finger over her mouth, signaling to Jordan that they should be as quiet as possible.

The door was slightly ajar, and she cautiously pushed it open. The hinges gave a loud creak as the door swung inward. The musty smell hit them immediately.

Inside, the old halls were covered in fading wallpaper, drop cloths, scaffolding, and a thick layer of dirt and dust.

Maeve saw a flicker of movement in the distance, and her heart rate spiked.

She couldn't help but feel a slight wave of dread wash over her, in the silence of the theater. She knew that they weren't alone.

As they made their way deeper into the theater, the sound of footsteps echoed through the corridors. Maeve's grip on her gun tightened as she rounded a corner.

People did desperate things when they were scared.

Why did Jordan have to tell her that ghost story? All she could picture was the pale face of a man who hadn't managed to escape.

Maeve and Jordan stepped through a pair of double doors to find row after row of chairs facing the main stage, their eyes scanning the room for any sign of Nick Stephenson. The dim lighting made it difficult to see. But she crept forward, until she made it all the way to the stage. Everything in sight was covered in a thick layer of dust.

"Where is he?" she said. Her gaze drifted back and forth to the cobwebs in the corners and the trash and stray pieces of rope left between the seats. Maeve's eyes eventually fell on a figure in the corner of the room.

Maeve recognized her as the assistant who had come to speak to Nick earlier that day. Vivian. Her dark hair framed her face, and tears ran down her eyes.

"Thank God you're here," she said, running forward as Maeve lowered her gun.

For a moment, Maeve couldn't make sense of her presence.

"You shouldn't be here," Maeve said. Something was strange about this girl. She just couldn't put her finger on what. But a part of her was relieved.

At least they knew that they had chosen the right place to look.

"Please, I just tried to help him. I knew he'd come here, and I tried to get him to turn himself in... but I think he's going crazy! He tried to hurt me... I'm scared."

"Why are you holding an old chair leg?" asked Jordan, looking down at the blunt object held in a white-knuckle grip in her hand.

"For protection. He tried to attack me. I'm afraid..."

"Just stay here," Maeve said, tightening her grip on the gun.

She would deal with Vivian later.

She stepped into one of the corridors off of the main part of the theater. Jordan followed close behind. Here, everything was even more rundown-- the red carpet was peeling up near the walls, and the wallpaper was coming off the plaster in shreds.

"Something is off with her," Maeve whispered over her shoulder to Jordan. "Something serious. I don't like it."

"She's a little too concerned about her friend," he agreed.

Maeve paced the hall slowly, turning quickly around each corner, ready at each moment to shoot.

But still, something didn't sit right.

How would she have known that Nick would come here? Why would she have come here herself, knowing it could put her in so much danger? If they were close, then maybe he told her about his relationships with the other three women. Maybe she would even have known where the hotel rooms were.

Maeve's thoughts were interrupted when she heard a faint sound coming from the end of the hall. She signaled to Jordan to follow her, and they made their way towards the sound.

It was coming from one of the dressing rooms, and Maeve's heart skipped a beat.

But still, she couldn't stop wondering about Vivian. Weren't her tears a little over the top?

A little bit manufactured?

Nick had been distressed, but not violent. He had claimed so adamantly that he didn't kill the three victims. Maeve had been so sure this was just another tactic, a way of gaining her sympathy. But what if…

"Of course," she realized, as all the pieces fell into place. "Vivian is the real killer. She's been playing with us this whole time."

As soon as Maeve said this, a dark figure burst out of the dressing room. Maeve almost shot her gun, afraid that this was another attacker. Her heart leapt up her throat, but soon the figure came into focus.

It was Nick.

He ran straight for the two detectives, hands held up in surrender.

"Please! You have to help me. She's trying to kill me!"

Maeve could see a nasty bruise on his forehead, and a deep cut that left blood dripping down one side of his face. His neck, also was marked with a red line, where a rope had been knotted around his throat.

“Stop!” said Jordan. “You’re under arrest!” He held his gun in Nick’s face, but Maeve quickly lowered her gun and gestured to Jordan to do the same.

“Wait. It all makes sense. She’s framing him, don’t you see?”

"Nick, calm down. We're here to help," said Maeve.

"Please, you have to help me. She's gone insane. I didn't do it, I swear," pleaded Nick, tears streaming down his face. Maeve could see the genuine fear in his eyes and, for the first time, she truly believed him.

"Alright, Nick. Tell us everything. What happened?" asked Jordan, his hand resting gently on Nick's shoulder.

Nick took a deep breath before beginning his tale, his words tumbling through the story.

"She was jealous. I think... of my success... of those women. And she killed them to get back at me. I didn't mean to take our show... I mean, we built it together, but I thought she understood. There could only be one..."

"Focus, Nick. You said she attacked you?"

"Yes. She met me at the precinct, told me to escape, and come here. I thought I could trust her, but when I arrived she was holding this rope, and she tried to strangle me."

“She was going to make it look like suicide,” Maeve guessed. "And we just left her downstairs.”

She could have kicked herself. She couldn't believe how careless she had been.

"We have to go back down there," Jordan said, his voice stern.

"You stay with Nick. I'm not making the same mistake twice."

Maeve quickly made her way back down the hall and descended the stairs, her gun held tightly in her hand. As she approached the door from which they had come, she heard soft footsteps approaching. She readied herself to fire, but when the figure came into view, she froze.

It was Vivian.

"Maeve, thank God," Vivian said, rushing forward and grasping Maeve's arm. "You have to help me."

Maeve pulled her arm away from Vivian's grip. "Don't touch me. We know it was you, Vivian. You killed those women and tried to frame Nick."

"You don't believe that madman, do you?" Vivian said. Maeve couldn't wrestle her arm free.

"It makes the most sense, doesn't it?" Maeve said. "You probably worked for over a decade on that show, and he didn't give you one ounce of credit. And more than that, he ignored you, chasing after shallow women, time and time again, didn't he?"

Vivian's expression faded into a hateful scowl. "You don't know anything about it."

"Come on, no one else has to get hurt. You can still make the right choice."

But Vivian pulled Maeve's arm so hard that she was forced to drop her gun. It clattered on the ground and fell away, on the other side of the room.

"We're way past that, Agent Sharp."

Vivian’s grip on Maeve’s arm tightened, and with one motion, she twisted Maeve’s wrist until pain shot up Maeve’s arm into her shoulder.

Maeve’s stomach sank.

This was a dangerous opponent to face unarmed.

She knew that she couldn't let Vivian get too close. Maeve quickly assessed the room for any way out, but all she could see was a window on the far wall. Maeve tried to back away slowly, keeping her eyes on Vivian.

"You don't have to do this, Vivian," Maeve said, trying to remain calm. "We can talk about this. We can get you help."

But Vivian wasn't listening. She kept her eyes fixed on Maeve.

She pulled a rope from the folds of her dress... a noose, Maeve realized.

Vivian lunged forward, and Maeve barely had time to slip away, retreating into the open doorway of a small room, crowded with moth-eaten costumes and old chairs.

Maeve looked up at Vivian and realized that she wasn't prepared for this fight, unarmed against this woman with nothing left to lose.

CHAPTER TWENTY SEVEN

Maeve remained silent, her eyes flicking to the noose and back to Vivian's face. Maeve didn't want to be caught in a fight with this woman, and she was still reeling from the knowledge that Vivian had almost bested her.

But she prepared herself to fight anyway, closing her fists and focusing on the woman in front of her.

Vivian chuckled, taking a step closer to Maeve.

"You know, I almost feel bad for you," she said, running a finger over the rough twine of the noose. "I'd say you were a step behind me this whole time, but you never managed to even get that close, did you?"

Maeve didn't respond, but felt a sense of rage rising within her.

In a way, Vivian was right.

Maeve had almost let all of Vivian's tricks blind her to the truth.

Her mind raced as she tried to come up with a plan. She looked around the room, searching for anything that could give her an advantage. The dusty props and broken furniture offered no help, and the only exit was blocked by Vivian.

"All this time, and you thought it was Nick? As though he's decisive enough to kill someone. He doesn't have the nerve."

Vivian stole a step closer.

Maeve's breath caught in her throat.

Her heart pounded in her chest as she tried to think of a way out.

She could feel the weight of the noose in Vivian's hand, the rough twine scraping against her skin. She knew that she had to act fast, or it would be too late.

She lunged forward, grabbing the noose from Vivian's hand. Vivian stumbled backward, caught off guard, and Maeve took the opportunity to strike.

But Vivian kept her grip tight on the rope in her hand, and Maeve couldn't manage to pull it free.

Then Vivian struck back.

She lunged forward, and tried to claw the noose over Maeve's head. Maeve felt the woman's long fingernails scratch her skin before the two pulled apart again.

But Maeve was trained for this, and she slipped away again, bobbing and weaving like she had been taught. She even managed to land a punch in Vivian's ribs, but this did little more than knock the breath out of her for a few short moments.

Even with Maeve's training, Vivian had a tenacity that was impossible to predict, an impulsive aggression. She fought like a rat trapped in a cage, with anger and fear, and determination.

The next time Vivian came at Maeve with that rope, Maeve didn't have any tricks up her sleeve. She was forced to play a game of cat and mouse, with Vivian chasing Maeve around the room.

Maeve dodged Vivian's next blow, forcing Vivian to stumble forward with the momentum. Maeve used the moment to spin around behind Vivian. She wrapped her arm around the woman's neck.

Maeve yanked back, using the crook of her elbow to press down on Vivian's neck.

She started to cough, but Maeve knew her place in the fight was as precarious as Vivian's.

Vivian was a smart woman, and she didn't take her title as an escape artist lightly.

Vivian struggled fiercely, and reached up and grabbed Maeve's hand. Maeve knew that with the right movement, Vivian could break her fingers.

With an even better one, she could dislocate her whole shoulder.

She waited for Vivian to pass out.

Moments felt like hours, but nothing happened.

Vivian's grip tightened on Maeve's hand.

She forced herself to drop the chokehold.

The two split apart, and Vivian brought a cautious hand to her neck…

She gasped, but looked up at Maeve with renewed hatred. Maeve's heart sank. She had missed her chance to incapacitate Vivian, and now she might never get it back.

Vivian shot forward again.

This time, when she tried to get the rope around Maeve's neck, she succeeded.

Before she could stop it, the rough material tightened around her neck.

All of a sudden, Maeve's breath was cut short.

A surge of fear took over her, as she tried uselessly to pull the rope away, to get a gasp of fresh air.

But Vivian pulled harder. And harder.

Maeve heard a garbled rasping sound, and realized that she was making it, a last attempt to call out for help. Her head pounded; she could hear her heartbeat and the sound of her lungs desperately trying to get air.

Until Maeve's vision started to turn black.

"You know," Vivian growled, her voice already distant and echoey. "My plan was to make it look like a suicide. But that will have to wait until after I've dealt with you."

The darkness in the corners of Maeve's vision grew, until she almost couldn't see anything.

Her head felt like it was going to explode. There was a ringing in her ears, until eventually the sound faded away.

All she could see was the face of Vivian, looking down at her with almost no expression written on her face. Not even anger. Only a clinical sort of focus.

Maeve's mind went blank. She had never been afraid of dying on the job, but she didn't think it would be like this.

Just as the darkness was closing in, she heard an enormous boom—and the door broke in.

Distracted, Vivian dropped the rope. There was enough slack for Maeve to breathe again.

She took in one desperate gasp, and the world came flooding back in.

The ringing in her ears stopped, and was replaced with the sound of her own coughing.

Jordan stood on the other side of the room with his gun drawn.

Maeve could tell that he was trying to decide if shooting at Vivian was too risky...if he missed, he could hit Maeve.

Vivian was clearly caught off guard by his arrival, pivoting between him and Maeve, still sitting in a crumpled heap on the floor, trying to regain her composure, to catch the breath she'd been deprived of.

"Drop the rope, Vivian," Jordan commanded. "It's over. You're under arrest for the murders of those women."

But Vivian wasn't going to give up now.

With a feral scream, Vivian lunged at Jordan. He fired his gun, but missed as Vivian's agility allowed her to move out of the way in time.

He dodged her attack and managed to get a hold of her arm, twisting it behind her back.

Vivian cried out in pain, but she refused to go down without a fight. She kicked at Jordan, trying to free herself from his hold, but he was too strong.

From the floor, Maeve couldn't believe what she was seeing.

The thought of Vivian actually succeeding in killing her sent shivers down her spine.

Vivian spat, and she cursed and clawed at Jordan’s face. He managed to get her into a chokehold too, but Vivian kicked and bit, threatening to break free and get away.

Maeve couldn’t let it happen.

And just when it looked like maybe she would overwhelm him too, Maeve managed to push herself to her feet. She wrapped Vivian’s legs in her own rope, forcing her to drop to the ground.

When she fell on the floor, Jordan didn't miss a moment.

He took the handcuffs from his belt and slapped them onto her wrists before she could get up again.

Maeve sank back to the floor, as she watched Vivian thrash like a writhing snake.

She stared blankly at the caught criminal, trying to process everything that had just happened. It all seemed like a dream, unreal and disconnected from reality.

But eventually, Maeve got up from the ground and looked around the room. Everything was still in disarray from their struggle—the table overturned, chairs knocked over, and the rope lying discarded on the ground.

Now that the moment had passed, and the adrenaline in her blood was quickly dissipating, she felt a tightness in her chest, a sudden surge of fear, and a sharp pain in her throat.

She wondered what would have happened if Jordan had not been there to help her.

She realized how blind she had been—following every lead except the one that ended at the actual culprit. But then again, Vivian had kept herself well hidden. She knew how to go unnoticed, ensured that all of her movements were untraceable, and beyond that, made the crime look like it had been committed by Nick.

She looked up at Jordan, who looked blankly back at her.

"I should have seen it sooner," she said.

"How could you have?"

Jordan looked down at the woman on the floor, who turned into a shell of the fearsome opponent she had been moments before.

"You'll regret this!" Vivian sputtered. But her thrashing turned into shuddering, and she started to cry as the defeat registered on her face.

"You'll—" she whimpered, her voice breaking. "You'll regret this. You will."

Jordan turned and looked at Maeve, who was still trying to find the strength to stand.

"Are you okay?" Jordan asked.

Before she could answer, they heard the sound of backup running down the hallway to find them.

Maeve let herself breathe a sigh of relief.

Vivian kicked and screamed as four men filed into the room to take her away. They had to lift her up completely as she refused to walk on her own.

Maeve's head swam, and for a few moments, she had to fight to stand again, fight against the pull of gravity, which seemed stronger than usual.

Then the two detectives followed their culprit out of the building, where a swarm of police cars and ambulances waited, along with Nick, who had found his way out of the building when Jordan left.

In the last moments of relative freedom, just before she was shut away in the police cruiser, Vivian caught Nick's attention. He was leaning on a police cruiser as the officers escorted her past him.

"You are nothing without me, do you understand?" Her face turned red with anger, the sound of her voice raised above the sound of the sirens. "You were only ever anything because *I* made you that way, because *I* am the better escape artist. I'll get out. And I'll come to find you. And all these cops won't be able to protect you when--"

The cops loaded her into a car, and Jordan shut the door, cutting her speech short.

EPILOGUE

Jordan found Maeve sitting on the back of an ambulance, with an EMT looking in her eyes, searching for the tell-tale signs of a concussion. The lights of the police cars nearby cast red and blue shadows on her face.

"How are you holding up?" he said, when the EMT stepped away to get another test.

Maeve took a deep breath, still feeling a tightness in her chest. Her hand rose to her throat, where a line of bruises was already forming.

"I'll be fine," she said. “I'm just a little shaken up.”

Jordan nodded, and leaned against the ambulance next to her. He took a package of cigarettes from his pocket, and offered her one.

Maeve shook her head; she had quit smoking years ago. But she watched as Jordan lit his own cigarette, and took a long drag.

"I should have seen it sooner," she said. No matter what she told herself, she kept returning to this thought.

Jordan shrugged, blowing a stream of smoke out from his mouth. "She was a smart one,” he said. “You did everything you could. A lesser detective would never have figured it out at all.”

Maeve nodded, knowing that even though the case was closed, she would never be able to shake the feeling of vulnerability that had taken hold of her.

"You caught her," he said. "That's what matters."

"It wasn't just me," Maeve admitted. She mustered a smile. "You were the one who thought to come here. I never would have remembered it if you hadn't said something."

He smirked. "Well, not everyone can be as intelligent and insightful as me in a pinch."

Maeve lightly punched his arm and rolled her eyes, but smiled so he would know she didn't mean it. "I don't think I thanked you. I don't know what would have happened if you hadn't..."

Her voice trailed off, as her expression faded to serious again. She thought of Vivian's noose looped tightly around her neck, how the world had been growing darker with each moment.

"I'm sure you would have figured something out," he said. "But still, you're welcome."

The EMT returned, and told Maeve that she was free to go.

"What now?" Jordan asked.

Maeve took a deep breath, thinking about how for every serial killer who ended up in prison like Vivian, there were ten that walked free.

"On to the next case, I guess. If you'll still be my partner."

"Oh, I'm happy to show you up on whatever case they put you on," he said. "But I really just was wondering what to do right now. Want to grab a beer? You look like you need one."

Maeve smiled, and shook her head. "I should get home. I have to visit my mother in the morning."

Jordan nodded. "Okay," he said. He squeezed her hand as she stood up, and wrapped her blazer around her shoulders. "Just take care of yourself, yeah?" he added. "The others in this city, the killers, they're not going to catch themselves."

Maeve smiled. "I'll see you Monday."

Knowing that everything was safely in the hands of the Vegas police, Maeve walked to the street corner and made her way back towards the main part of the strip. She knew that she shouldn't, but she wanted to take it in one last time.

The lights had a sinister glow, as she looked up into the flashing signs and glowing fountains.

This place was full of people like Vivian. And worse.

But the rest would have to wait for another day.

When she couldn't walk any farther, she called a cab, and went home.

***

Maeve sat at her mother's bedside, holding her mom's wrinkled hand. Her mother drifted in and out of consciousness all day, but this was a moment of clarity. Her long silver hair had been freshly brushed and fell over her shoulders in waves.

She looked insubstantial under the piles of blankets and quilts, surrounded with beeping machines that the hospice nurses had added. The room had almost been turned into its own hospital, full of pill bottles, heart monitors, and a nurse running in and out every few moments to check on her.

After such a difficult case, Maeve was glad she could finally be at her mother's side. But at the same time, it was hard to see her like this, growing weaker by the moment. She had to suppress the tears that threatened to fall down her cheeks.

Maeve's mother smiled weakly at her daughter, her ice-blue eyes meeting Maeve's brown ones. "Thank you for coming, dear," she said, her voice raspy and weak.

Maeve clutched her mother's hand tightly. "Of course, Mom. I wouldn't be anywhere else."

They sat in silence for a few moments, listening to the machines beep steadily in the background.

Maeve couldn't help but feel a sense of sadness as she watched her mother fade away slowly. Maeve remembered her mom as the most vibrant woman she'd known, constantly running from one thing to the next.

"How's work?" her mother asked, her voice barely above a whisper.

Maeve smiled softly, trying to put on a brave face. She had covered the bruises on her neck in concealer so that no one would notice. "It's good, Mom. We solved a big case yesterday."

There was a dim light in her mother's eyes when she said that.

"I'm proud of you," she said, her voice barely above a whisper.

A tear ran down Maeve's face, as she looked down at her mother, too weak to sit up.

"But you didn't have to--"

"Mom, don't," Maeve tried to stop for her.

"You didn't have to come all the way back for me. I know what it means to you... this place. I know what it means to all of us."

"You thought about leaving too?"

"Of course. But in the end, I didn't want to sell the house, and see that..." her mother's voice broke. "I didn't want her to come back here, looking for us, only to find that we weren't there anymore. Promise me, you won't sell the house when I'm gone. You don't have to live in it, but just don't..."

"Of course, Mom. Anything you want," said Maeve, feeling her own voice break. She wished she could get closure for her mom, to finally find out what happened to Veronica.

"I tried to get Dad to come too, but he..."

She was cut off with the sound of footsteps coming up the stairs. They were heavy, familiar, almost energetic.

Then her father appeared in the doorway.

"Dad!" she said. In spite of everything that happened, and the last words that they had spoken to each other, Maeve was so happy and surprised to see him that she shot up from her chair and hugged him.

He smelled the same, of alcohol and tobacco, but at least he was there.

"Hey, kiddo," he said, in his usual gruff tone. "Heard you closed a big case. First week back. That's good work."

Maeve thanked him, and returned to the bedside.

"Cynthia," he said, looking down at her mother.

Maeve wondered how many years it had been since the two were even in the same room together— it had to have been at least since her graduation from the academy, but even then, she couldn't remember if they had looked at each other.

He must have been even more struck by how different she looked, how frail and tired.

"Bill," she said. Though she was surprised, Maeve could tell that this visit meant a lot to her. That they had been through enough together for him to come to her side now.

Her dad stood there—silent. He didn't know what else to say.

"I wish that your brother was here," her mother whispered. "I wish..."

"That reminds me," her dad said. "I got you something."

He went into the hallway, and returned with an iPad.

"Bill, you know I can't use this," Maeve's mother said.

"Just turn it on, won't you?"

Maeve saw that the Lock Screen had been preloaded with a picture of their family—their complete family—all five of them standing on the edge of the Grand Canyon when they were little.

"What's this?" she said, when she unlocked it, finding that a Skype call was already underway.

"I pulled a few strings."

Then her brother's face appeared on the screen.

He had angled himself so that his mother wouldn't have to see the prison bars behind him, or much of his orange jumpsuit.

"You're here!" she said.

"Sorry I can't be there in person, Mom. I wish I could. But I want you to know that I'm thinking of you, and I'm here for you."

Maeve knew that her father must have pulled some strings to get him here, even virtually.

Cynthia burst into tears and hugged Maeve. No longer able to restrain herself, Maeve found herself crying too.

Was this what she had needed all along? Reconciliation with her family?

They stayed like that all afternoon, the four of them, just comforting Maeve's mother.

Once they had cried and reminisced for a long time, Maeve and her father walked out of the room, to allow her mother more time to rest. Maeve wanted to spend more time together, but she was already drifting asleep, unable to keep her eyes open.

The two of them stood in the entryway, of the house, and her father said, "I never thought I'd come back here."

Maeve allowed herself a grim smile.

And then he leaned in close and spoke to Maeve in a low whisper.

"Maeve, you have to find her."

At first, Maeve was too shocked to respond.

"I have to give up. I was never as good as you are now, in all my years on the force. I couldn't find her..." his voice trailed off, and it sounded like he was about to cry. "I... failed my daughter. But that doesn't mean you will."

"Dad, what are you saying?" Maeve asked, looking up into his eyes, which were turning red and filling with tears.

"You have to find out what happened to Veronica. Before your mother passes. I know I didn't do much for her when we were together, but I think it would help her."

Maeve pressed her lips together.

Of course she had always spent her nights thinking about her sister's case, and wondering what the police had missed. She had always planned to one day return to the files and find out for herself.

But she didn't think that today was that day.

"A few years ago, I found something in her things," he said. "It could be something, after the case has been cold for so long. I want to give it to you."

Maeve's own tears returned as she stepped out the front door, without another word.

Maybe her father was right. He couldn't find Veronica. But she could.

She had to.

NOW AVAILABLE!

WITH ENVY
(A Maeve Sharp FBI Suspense Thriller—Book Two)

FBI Special Agent Maeve Sharp, a rising star in the BAU, decides to leave behind a shining career when she transfers to Las Vegas to come back home to her dying mother and incarcerated brother. But when victims of a new killer appear on the strip, all with chronic gambling problems, Maeve digs deeper, and in a shocking twist, realizes that this killer is not at all what he seems….

"A brilliant book. I couldn't put it down and I never guessed who the murderer was!"
—Reader review for Only Murder

WITH ENVY is book #2 in a new series by #1 bestselling and critically acclaimed mystery and suspense author Rylie Dark, whose books have received over 2,000 five-star reviews and ratings.

FBI Special Agent Maeve Sharp never got over her sister's disappearance when they were teenagers, the case gone cold, the feeling that just maybe she is still out there, somewhere. It ruined her family and destroyed her father who, once a decorated cop on the LVPD, now sits alone in a dilapidated trailer in the middle of nowhere, refusing to reconcile with her. It wrecked her brother, too, leading to lockup after lockup, as he pleads with Maeve to help get her out. And it wrecked her mom most of all, who in her dying days can think of nothing else.

Maeve though she got away from it all when she transferred to Quantico and made a career for herself.

But the past has a way of calling, of bringing back dark and unresolved memories. And Maeve has stepped right back into, ready, this time, to wrestle her darkest demons while she hunts down new serial killers….

A cat-and-mouse thriller with harrowing twists and turns and filled with heart-pounding suspense, the MAEVE SHARP mystery series offers a fresh twist on the genre as it introduces two brilliant protagonists who will make you fall in love and keep you turning pages late into the night.

Future books in the series are also available.

"I loved this thriller, read it in one sitting. Lots of twists and turns and I didn't guess the
culprit at all… Already pre-ordered the second!"
—Reader review for Only Murder

"This book takes off with a bang… An excellent read, and I'm looking forward to the next book!"
—Reader review for SEE HER RUN

"Fantastic book! It was hard to put down. I can't wait to see what happens next!"
—Reader review for SEE HER RUN

"The twists and turns kept coming. Can't wait to read the next book!"
—Reader review for SEE HER RUN

"A must-read if you enjoy action-packed stories with good plots!"
—Reader review for SEE HER RUN

"I really like this author and this series starts with a bang. It will keep you turning the pages till the end of the book and wanting more."
—Reader review for SEE HER RUN

"I can't say enough about this author! How about 'out of this world'! This author is going to go far!"
—Reader review for ONLY MURDER

"I really enjoyed this book… The characters were alive, and the twists and turns were great. It will keep you reading till the end and leave you wanting more."
—Reader review for NO WAY OUT

"This is an author that I highly recommend. Her books will have you begging for more."
—Reader review for NO WAY OUT

Rylie Dark

Bestselling author Rylie Dark is author of the SADIE PRICE FBI SUSPENSE THRILLER series, comprising six books; of the CARLY SEE FBI SUSPENSE THRILLER series, comprising six books; of the MIA NORTH FBI SUSPENSE THRILLER series, comprising six books (and counting); of the MORGAN STARK FBI SUSPENSE THRILLER series, comprising five books; of the HAILEY ROCK FBI SUSPENSE THRILLER series, comprising five books (and counting); of the TARA STRONG MYSTERY series, comprising five books (and counting); of the ALEX QUINN FBI SUSPENSE THRILLER series, comprising five books (and counting); and of the MAEVE SHARP FBI SUSPENSE THRILLER, comprising five books (and counting).

An avid reader and lifelong fan of the mystery and thriller genres, Rylie loves to hear from you, so please feel free to visit www.ryliedark.com to learn more and stay in touch.

BOOKS BY RYLIE DARK

MAEVE SHARP FBI SUSPENSE THRILLER
WITH MALICE (Book #1)
WITH ENVY (Book #2)
WITH VENGEANCE (Book #3)
WITH RAGE (Book #4)
WITH YOU (Book #5)

ALEX QUINN SUSPENSE THRILLER
FIRST, MURDER (Book #1)
SECOND, DEATH (Book #2)
THIRD, ENVY (Book #3)
FOURTH, LUST (Book #4)
FIFTH, WRATH (Book #5)

TARA STRONG MYSTERY
GIRL WITHOUT A CHANCE (Book #1)
GIRL WITHOUT A HOME (Book #2)
GIRL WITHOUT A TRACE (Book #3)
GIRL WITHOUT A NAME (Book #4)
GIRL WITHOUT A PRAYER (Book #5)

HAILEY ROCK FBI SUSPENSE THRILLER
BEHIND YOU (Book #1)
BESIDE YOU (Book #2)
AFTER YOU (Book #3)
WATCHING YOU (Book #4)
JUDGING YOU (Book #5)

SADIE PRICE FBI SUSPENSE THRILLER
ONLY MURDER (Book #1)
ONLY RAGE (Book #2)
ONLY HIS (Book #3)
ONLY ONCE (Book #4)
ONLY SPITE (Book #5)
ONLY MADNESS (Book #6)

MIA NORTH FBI SUSPENSE THRILLER
SEE HER RUN (Book #1)
SEE HER HIDE (Book #2)
SEE HER SCREAM (Book #3)
SEE HER VANISH (Book #4)
SEE HER GONE (Book #5)
SEE HER DEAD (Book #6)

CARLY SEE FBI SUSPENSE THRILLER
NO WAY OUT (Book #1)
NO WAY BACK (Book #2)
NO WAY HOME (Book #3)
NO WAY LEFT (Book #4)
NO WAY UP (Book #5)
NO WAY TO DIE (Book #6)

MORGAN STARK FBI SUSPENSE THRILLER
TOO LATE (Book #1)
TOO CLOSE (Book #2)
TOO FAR GONE (Book #3)
TOO LOST (Book #4)
TOO BROKEN (Book #5)

Printed in Great Britain
by Amazon

43229402R00086